F

SPECIAL MESSAGE TO READERS

THE ULVERSCROFT FOUNDATION
(registered UK charity number 264873)

was established in 1972 to provide funds for research, diagnosis and treatment of eye diseases. Examples of major projects funded by the Ulverscroft Foundation are:-

- The Children's Eye Unit at Moorfields Eye Hospital, London
- The Ulverscroft Children's Eye Unit at Great Ormond Street Hospital for Sick Children
- Funding research into eye diseases and treatment at the Department of Ophthalmology, University of Leicester
- The Ulverscroft Vision Research Group, Institute of Child Health
- Twin operating theatres at the Western Ophthalmic Hospital, London
- The Chair of Ophthalmology at the Royal Australian College of Ophthalmologists

You can help further the work of the Foundation by making a donation or leaving a legacy. Every contribution is gratefully received. If you would like to help support the Foundation or require further information, please contact:

THE ULVERSCROFT FOUNDATION
The Green, Bradgate Road, Anstey
Leicester LE7 7FU, England
Tel: (0116) 236 4325
website: www.foundation.ulverscroft.com

FIRE ON THE MOON

On vacation at her aunt's villa in Portugal, Jennifer is attracted to both Neil and Philip Alenquer, two brothers who live in an old castle overlooking the sea. But Jennifer soon senses that something is wrong, though it is not clear where the intangible clues are leading. Words left unsaid; the burnt-out shell of a cottage; terror in response to the recitation of a poem; gunshots on the beach. It is a mystery with potentially deadly consequences, as Jennifer and her aunt learn when an arsonist sets the villa alight . . .

V. J. BANIS

FIRE ON
THE MOON

Complete and Unabridged

LINFORD
Leicester

First published in Great Britain

First Linford Edition
published 2015

A catalogue record for this book is available
from the British Library.

ISBN 978–1–4448–2626–5

Published by
F. A. Thorpe (Publishing)
Anstey, Leicestershire

Set by Words & Graphics Ltd.
Anstey, Leicestershire
Printed and bound in Great Britain by
T. J. International Ltd., Padstow, Cornwall

This book is printed on acid-free paper

1

I suppose the moment I stepped from the plane in the Lisbon airport, I should have had a premonition that I wasn't going to have the perfect vacation to which I had so long looked forward. Carlotta was not at the airport when I arrived, and the weather was unreasonably gloomy, the sky dark and threatening rain — an unusual phenomenon, I learned later, for a Portuguese May. I was too excited, however, to think about dreary weather, and my parents had warned me that Carlotta was prone to absent-mindedness. So the slight disappointments went by almost unnoticed.

I doubt if anything could have succeeded in dampening my spirits. This was my first trip to Europe — my first trip to anywhere for that matter, and minor disappointments could not overcome my excitement. I'd spent most of the flight imagining myself lolling on Carlotta's terrace, watching the Atlantic wash its beaches in preparation for the swarm of tourists due later in the month. I thought it was to be a dream vacation with Aunt Carlotta.

I joined the rest of the passengers from the plane in boarding the little buses that waited to take us to the customs shed. I kept peering out of the bus window to see if I could catch a glimpse of Carlotta's face among those waiting on the other side of the fence. She wasn't there, but taking the dismal weather into consideration, I couldn't blame her for not standing out in the cold. She was most likely inside the terminal waiting for me to get through the business of customs.

I paused in the crush of passengers beside the customs barrier and strained to look over their heads. I didn't see her; but not seeing her still did not disturb me much. I knew my parents were right; Carlotta was a bit scatterbrained at times, so I guess subconsciously I was prepared for the possibility of her having forgotten my arrival time. Knowing her, she would — sooner or later — come rushing into the terminal all out of breath, make a simple apology, and that would be that. She wouldn't go on and on apologizing until her apology became artificial. There was nothing artificial about Carlotta. She was sometimes flighty and illogical, yet her common sense and sound advice had helped me overcome my despair after Andrew Fuller broke our engagement. It had also been Carlotta who had cautioned me about the kind of young man who turned out to be more interested in my family's money than in me. I loved Carlotta for her strengths as well as her weaknesses; I suppose she reminded me a bit of myself.

So now, here I was at last in Portugal, surrounded by clusters of dark, foreign-looking people all chattering away in languages I couldn't understand a word of. I stood in the center of the main terminal for I don't know how long, and carefully watched for Carlotta. But by the time a half hour had gone by, part of my excitement had gone with it.

I can't continue just to sit here and do nothing, I told myself. *Face facts,*

Jennifer. Carlotta forgot, or she got tied up. Go telephone. Do something.

Of course — the telephone. I stood and glanced around. There was a row of very American-looking telephone booths near the main entrance. I could leave my bags where they were and keep an eye both on them and on the main entrance, in case Carlotta came bustling in while I was at the telephone.

I'd had enough foresight to exchange some of my dollars for escudos before leaving Kennedy Airport. I supposed the telephone systems in Europe operated on much the same principle as our own. There was a little sign over the instrument which I took to be instructions for operating the telephone; unfortunately it was not printed in English.

I took out my small assortment of unfamiliar coins and deposited the only one that fit the slot — assuming that it had to be the right one. I waited. I dialed 'O' and waited some more. Nothing happened. I jiggled the hook a few times. Nothing. Reluctantly I replaced the receiver and waited for the funny little coin to be returned. It wasn't.

I picked up the Lisbon directory, but I knew before I looked up Carlotta's name that she would not be listed. She had told me that her villa was some distance from Lisbon — or *Lisboa* as she had called it.

I decided I needed some help. I glanced over at my suitcases. They were still there, untouched. I studied the people moving through the terminal. My gaze fell on a man walking slowly back and forth near the exit. He was wearing a uniform with a badge. Surely he would know how to operate a Portuguese telephone.

I stepped directly into his path. 'Do you speak English?' I asked brightly.

He smiled and touched his fingers to the brim of his cap. '*Si*, senhorita. A little.'

'Good,' I said, trying not to sound anxious. 'I wonder if you would help me?'

'If I can.' His accent was charming.

'My aunt was supposed to meet me but she hasn't shown up. I thought I would telephone her but I can't seem to operate the telephone.'

His smile broadened. 'Ah, *si*. Permit me.'

He stepped up to the telephone and took out what appeared to be a New York subway token. He dropped it into the same little slot that had swallowed up my coin. He pushed a little plunger, which I hadn't seen before, then muttered something into the mouthpiece. He turned and asked me for my aunt's name and address.

Quickly I rummaged in my handbag and pulled out her last letter. I pointed to the neatly written return address. The man repeated the name and address into the telephone. I waited. Another jumble of unfamiliar words followed. He covered the mouthpiece with his hand and said, 'The operator will look up the number and put your call through.'

'Thank you,' I said with relief and gratitude.

He spoke into the mouthpiece again. The language sounded so soft and gentle. All the words sounded more like music than spoken dialogue.

'It is — ah — how you say — ringing,' he said finally.

He held the receiver pressed lightly

against his ear and waited for a long time. Again he spoke into the mouthpiece then replaced the receiver. 'The operator says that there is no answer,' he said, looking very apologetic. 'I am sorry.'

I shrugged and tried not to look disappointed. 'She is most likely on her way here,' I said.

He handed me the 'subway token' that had dropped into the return slot when he replaced the receiver. 'If you need to call again, senhorita, use this. Tell the operator who you wish to speak to and she will get the number for you,' he assured me. 'Sometimes they do not speak good English like me, but if you talk slowly they will understand.' His smile was infectious. 'Now,' he said, giving me a polite bow, 'can I help you further?'

'Oh, thank you, no,' I said. 'You have been very kind.' I wondered if I was supposed to tip him. I decided a tip might insult his gallantry. I put out my hand. He took it, and to my surprise turned it palm down and touched it to his lips. I felt my face turn scarlet. He smiled again, turned, and went back to his post by the doors.

Now what? I asked myself as I walked slowly back to my luggage. I decided on a taxi. I looked up at the wall clock. My episode with the telephone had taken up another ten minutes. My feet hurt and I didn't want to think about my empty stomach. I had been too excited to eat on the flight over. There was, I supposed, some sort of eating place tucked away in the terminal, but I just did not feel up to trying to decipher a Portuguese menu, especially after my failure with the telephone.

I looked down at my pile of suitcases. I'd need a porter.

'Senhorita!'

The man so startled me I jumped. He had come up behind me and had said 'senhorita' more in the tone of a command than a greeting.

I turned sharply and found myself facing a surly-looking individual dressed in a shabby waistcoat and formless trousers, the bottoms of which were stuffed into battered, mud-caked boots. By the look of him, he had apparently dressed in a hurry and had given little concern as to what he had put on. He was in his mid-thirties, I guessed, and far from unattractive — tall, with an olive complexion and black, curly hair, grown a little longer than I normally like, but very becoming. I noticed that he held his head at a peculiar angle — tilted slightly down and away from me. I thought he must have a kink in his neck.

The expression on his face was as unattractive as his clothes. He appeared to be very angry at something or someone, and by the way he scowled at me I got the distinct impression that it was I with whom he was angry. Looking at him slightly unnerved me.

I smiled brightly and said, 'Yes.'

'Are you Jennifer Carter?' He didn't smile. On the contrary, his mouth pulled down at the corners and he looked fiercer than before. His eyes narrowed and he gave me a look that said I had better be Jennifer Carter if I knew what was good for me. There was something overbearing in his attitude. I had always had a particular dislike for people who tried to dominate, especially men who considered themselves superior to women. Here was one such man, I decided, and I didn't like him.

I tilted back my head and purposely let my smile fade. 'Yes, I'm Jennifer Carter,' I said, meeting his coldness with a coldness of my own. 'Why?'

His scowl deepened. His gaze did not falter. 'Your aunt sent me for you. She had to go to Paris.' His English was as clipped and as uncordial as his eyes. He made it very clear that he hadn't been pleased about having to come for me. 'Are those yours?' He glanced down at my pile of luggage. The glance and the inflection of voice made my suitcases seem even shabbier than they were. He didn't wait for me to answer yes or no but reached down and gathered up the suitcases. They were far from light, yet he picked them up as though they weighed nothing at all.

'Hey, wait a mi — '

'This way.' He turned his back and started away.

My first impulse was to refuse to follow. He had all the friendliness of a cobra. He never glanced back to see if I was behind him.

My stubbornness gave way to common sense. I shrugged. After all, Carlotta had obviously sent him.

I caught up with him just as he reached the door leading out of the terminal. I thought for a moment that he was going to wait and hold the door open for me, but he did not. Neither did he offer any assistance in crossing the busy street. I had to keep one eye out for careening cars and the other on him.

We crossed — with some difficulty on my part — to a large, old, black limousine. It was a relic — but although it had seen better days it still had an aura of elegance.

He wasn't a chauffeur; that was made plain by the way he threw my luggage just inside the back seat, making it necessary for me to go around to the other side of the car to get in. I had hardly closed the door before he started up the car and pulled straight out into the heavy stream of traffic. There was an instant blast of horns as we lurched recklessly away from

11

the curb; he hadn't looked in either direction to see if the way were clear. We suffered no consequences, but I kept a firm grip on my handbag and secretly hoped the trip would be a short one. I found it necessary to keep reminding myself that Aunt Carlotta had, after all, sent this man for me. He must be someone she knew, or perhaps employed.

I forced myself to be unconcerned and tried to relax against the soft, worn upholstery. I sighed and contented myself with the thought that I was on my way to Carlotta's villa and that was all that really mattered at the moment.

He drove fast, but expertly. I tried to concentrate on the passing scenery. My first glimpse of Europe. Strange, but it mostly went by unnoticed. The excitement I had felt about coming here had been wiped out by this one dour, unfriendly man. He hadn't succeeded in completely taking the joy out of my arrival, but he hadn't made it pleasant.

My gaze wandered from the window to the back of his head. Despite my disapproval of his manners, I nevertheless found my interest drawn to him and not to the outskirts of Lisbon through which we were passing.

'Did you say my aunt was in Paris?' I ventured.

He nodded.

'When will she be returning?'

He shrugged his shoulders and said nothing.

The strong, silent type, I thought. I realized too late that he hadn't seen my smile when I said, 'Are you always this quiet, or are you just being so for my benefit?'

He didn't answer — then suddenly a taxi swerved and cut directly in front of us. My driver slammed on the brakes and the limousine lurched to one side, toppling me and my luggage down onto the floor of the back seat. I was positive we were going to turn over, but my sullen friend proved a more than capable driver. He righted the car, leaned out the window, and let out what I took to be a solid stream of Portuguese profanity.

As I lay in an uncomfortable huddle on the floor I felt the car slow down. I thought he was going to stop to help me right myself and my bags. I was wrong. He merely slowed for a left-hand turn, and continued on in unconcerned silence. I frowned at his back as I reseated myself, intending to give him a piece of my mind.

The words never came. I saw the left side of his face for the first time and I had to stifle a gasp. A hideous scar ran the length of his cheek — from cheekbone almost to the line of his chin. Quickly I looked away. When I looked back I found myself being stared at in the rear-view mirror. His eyes were thin slivers of ice. I forced my eyes away and felt the car go a little faster. I couldn't say anything. I looked out the window, but all my eyes could see was that horrible scar. I could feel him watching me in the rear-view mirror. My eyes were drawn to it like a magnet. Our gazes met and held for a moment. He lowered his eyes and fixed them on the road ahead. The tilt was gone from his head. He held it straight and proud.

Minutes before I had disliked this man; now I pitied him, although I sensed that

that was the one thing he would despise most. I wanted to apologize for my earlier remark. I wanted to say something, anything, just to show that his unfortunate disfigurement didn't matter. I wanted him to feel that I understood. Unfortunately, whatever I said would only bring attention to the one thing he wanted to forget. The reason for his rude, unfriendly behavior seemed plain enough now, but it was too late to tell him so. He had seen the look of horror on my face; he had heard my stifled gasp; he knew I had been repulsed when I had seen the left side of his face. Strangely enough, however, now that the initial shock was over, I didn't feel repulsion.

By now we had left Lisbon far behind and were heading southwest toward the ocean. I could smell it in the air. I rolled down the window and let the wind, thick with the smell of salt, clear my thoughts. We rounded a sweeping curve in the road and there before me lay the most beautiful sight I had ever seen, and one I will never forget.

The bleached sand, dotted with patches

of rock and moss, hugged the Atlantic like a jealous mistress. Here and there pastel cottages sat in the midst of little fenced gardens. The sun was high, and the sky — now solidly blue and unclouded — blended so perfectly with the lovely blue water that the line of horizon was indistinguishable. High mountains towered on one side of the road, their tops crowned with trees and lush, velvety shrubs.

I stared in wonder at the exquisite contrast between quiet isolation and teeming vitality. Summer waters broke winter-white against the beach; flat, creamy sands swept high into towering cliffs of green; square, low houses stretched up to touch the sky with their tapered, filigreed chimneys. The smell of oranges, lemons, grapes, and almonds mingled deliciously with the fresh sea air.

It was the paradise I had always sought. I hadn't the faintest idea what this place was called, or how far we had to travel. And I didn't care. It was too beautiful.

'Magnificent, isn't it?' I asked, hypnotized by the beauty of the landscape, completely forgetting what had gone before.

His silence suddenly brought memory back. Our eyes met again in the mirror. This time it was I who lowered my gaze.

2

We drove until the sun dipped slightly to the west. The dreary weather that had greeted me when I arrived was gone. Neither I nor the surly man in front of me spoke a word. From time to time we regarded each other in the rear-view mirror, but that was our only communication.

I found him looking at me again. This time I gave him a nervous smile. I decided the long period of silence had to come to an end. I was becoming too uneasy.

'You have me at a disadvantage,' I said as brightly as I could manage. 'You know my name, but unfortunately I do not know yours.'

Long pause, then: 'Neil.'

My heart gave a little tug. He was going to come out of his shell.

'Are you a friend of my aunt's?'

I saw his shoulders sag slightly and was

sure I'd won the battle over silence. I waited. But he said no more. He simply pressed down harder on the accelerator.

His stubbornness only served to increase my nervousness, and unfortunately when I'm nervous I usually find myself tempted to talk in order to alleviate my discomfort. I flattered Portugal, the scenery, the people I'd noticed at the airport, the polite man in uniform who had helped me with the telephone. I talked about Michigan, the vastness of the New York airport, the smoothness of the flight over. I tried to overlook his silence.

I was careful not to ask any more direct questions. I knew he'd only ignore them. Furthermore, I was careful not to say anything too personal, concerning either myself or him.

'I had no idea my aunt lived so far from the city,' I said as we made a sharp turn off the main road and started up the side of a mountain.

'We are nearly there,' he said.

I almost didn't believe my ears. He had actually volunteered an entire sentence. I felt my verbosity had paid off. I smiled to myself and leaned back in the seat, content.

And we were nearly there. After a few minutes' drive up a very steep road we leveled off atop a high bluff. I gazed out at the vast Atlantic. Somewhere out there, farther than I could imagine, was the world I'd left behind. I suddenly wanted to rush back to it. Despite the exquisite beauty of Portugal, I had a strange foreboding. I wanted to return to where I knew everything to be secure and safe and friendly.

As we skirted the edge of the cliff I found myself turning to stare at the back of the man's head — Neil's head. Was he representative of what Portuguese men were like? I hoped not. Who was he? I wondered. Did he live at Carlotta's villa?

As I thought about these questions, he swerved into a driveway and drove between two giant stone posts that supported intricately wrought iron gates, up a gravel drive and into a spacious courtyard. I was stunned by the beauty of the villa. It was the lightest of pinks, with a peaked roof of a darker hue. A marble terrace ran the full length of the lovely old house. The terrace was dotted with potted cypress trees. Tall French windows blinked at me as I got out of the limousine. Their shutters were open and fastened to the flat façade. I had known that Carlotta lived well, but I had hardly expected such luxury. The lawns were freshly manicured; obviously they received loving care. It was an enchanting place. The moment I saw it I completely forgot my feeling of foreboding and my anxiety to return home. Now I was eager to rush inside.

Neil took my bags from the back seat and stacked them near the front door. He rummaged around in a flower pot, produced a key and unlocked the door, and stepped aside for me. I went through into the cool luxury of the interior but Neil remained outside. I heard him move my bags immediately inside the foyer. I was so captivated by the beauty of the house that I hardly heard the door close. I was sure Neil was standing behind me, but then I heard the car's motor roar and speed down the drive and away.

Quickly I went back outside. The car was just disappearing down the drive. I shook my head and started back into the villa. The key was in the latch. I took it out and dropped it into my purse. 'What a strange man,' I said to the emptiness of the foyer. At least he had brought me here, and for that I was very grateful.

A long, sweeping staircase led from the foyer to the floor above. I glanced at my bags and decided I was too weary and hungry to bother carting them upstairs. Anyway, I had no idea where to put them after I did lug them up.

I crossed the foyer, listening to the echo of my heels on the black and white marble squares. 'Anybody home?' I called.

No answer. I went down several steps that led into what I thought must be the 'lair' Carlotta spoke so fondly of. It was a beautiful room, bright and feminine, and not very well organized. Carlotta's sketches were everywhere, and her award-winning dress designs were framed and hung in a cluster on one high wall. An easel and a drawing board stood before one bank of windows, isolated somewhat from the rest of the room, and their rough, natural wood contrasted sharply with the highly polished, exquisitely carved French antiques on the deep-pile rug. The lair was massive clutter, but exquisite clutter.

I took my time inspecting the room. I wondered about servants. Surely Carlotta didn't keep up this magnificent place all by herself. It was much too large, and by the look of it, was cared for quite regularly. Everything seemed in its proper place. Even the fabric swatches were neatly stacked.

I half-expected a note or message of some kind but I saw none. I crossed the foyer and found the living room, which far outshone the lair. Unlike the lair, the living room was exclusively Spanish — Portuguese, I corrected. In spite of its massive furniture, it exuded warmth and intimacy. A huge fireplace dominated one wall. Twin sofas upholstered in an elaborate but tasteful brocade flanked the hearth. It was somehow masculine, yet delicately feminine. It was like Carlotta herself — a paradox, a lovely paradox.

When I turned I saw the note propped

on the refectory table just inside the door. Towering above the slip of paper was a handsome porcelain vase holding a huge spray of yellow flowers.

'Jen, Make yourself at home. Sorry I couldn't meet you but I asked Philip Alenquer to pick you up. Isn't he a love? I should be back from Paris around six. Philip will see that you're entertained, I'm sure.
Love, C.'

The man who met me had said his name was Neil. I frowned. I scanned the note again. 'Philip Alenquer.' Carlotta had written it quite clearly. And I absolutely could not agree that he was a 'love' as Carlotta had written. Something got mixed up along the way, I decided, as I folded the note and tossed it into the waste-basket.

I shrugged; Carlotta would straighten it all out when she got here. Six o'clock, she'd said. I glanced at my watch. It was only a little after three.

The time suddenly reminded me that I

hadn't eaten anything substantial all day. I'd take Carlotta at her word. 'Make yourself at home,' she'd said. My hunger convinced me to do just that. I went in search of a kitchen.

A lovely formal dining room brought me to a serving pantry and finally into a large kitchen, very modern and equipped with the latest conveniences. It was spotless, and the refrigerator was virtually bursting with all sorts of good things to eat. I slipped out of my suit jacket, rolled up the sleeves of my blouse and went to work. It took a while to search out everything — bread, seasonings, dishes, napkin — and by the time I'd fixed myself an omelet and toast, made the coffee and set a place in the breakfast nook, I was truly ravenous.

As I sat relishing my meal, I noticed another terrace just beyond the window, at the back of the villa. It was white with a pink balustrade and overlooked the ocean from the cliff on which it was perched. At one end was a long flight of wooden steps leading down to a private beach. One look at the terrace told me how I would spend the afternoon. The sun was hot and inviting. I could afford some exposure to the sun. My skin was far too pale compared with the dark-skinned natives of Portugal. And there was that book I hadn't glanced at once on the flight over.

I finished eating, rinsed the dishes and put away all evidence of my culinary efforts. I felt better. My body ached less, and my step was a bit springier as I walked back into the foyer and picked up my small overnight case.

Upstairs I found three bedrooms. The one with the study/sitting room was obviously Carlotta's. The one adjoining I took to be mine because there were flowers and a bowl of fruit on a low table. I intended to don a swim suit and get some sun, but I remembered that my swimsuit was in the large bag and I didn't feel much like going back downstairs and lugging it up right now. Instead, feeling a bit daring, I slipped into a short nightdress and made my way down to the rear terrace, uttering a silent prayer that no one would discover me in my slightly scandalous attire.

The sun was as warm and wonderful as I had imagined it. Far below me the waters of the Atlantic lapped and soothed the shore. I was tempted to climb down the wooden steps to the beach, but considering my apparel, thought better of it. I pulled a chaise into the direct sunlight and stretched out on it, then picked up my book, but couldn't concentrate on the first sentence. Neil whatever-his-name crept into my thoughts. I suddenly realized how reckless I'd been getting into a strange car with a man I'd never seen before. Anything could have happened to me. Perhaps Carlotta didn't know Neil at all. Who on earth was he? Obviously Carlotta hadn't intended him to meet me. Why did he?

I couldn't see that it made much difference now, though. I was safe and sound. And the sun was being unreasonably kind. It proved to be the friend I needed just then. My head nodded, my muscles relaxed and I closed my eyes. I slept.

A buzzing interrupted my sleep. My eyes flew open. The sky was darker, the air crisper and less comfortable. I shivered, pulling my night dress down over my knees.

The buzzing came again. Someone was ringing the doorbell. I jumped to my feet and hurried from the terrace. I couldn't answer the door in the outfit I was wearing. I dashed up the stairs, glancing at my watch as I went.

It was almost five. Surely it wasn't Carlotta; she would have her own key. But then I thought of the key in the potted cypress — the one I'd dropped into my handbag. Possibly Carlotta didn't carry a key and relied upon that one.

I went to the window of the bedroom and looked down onto the front terrace. It wasn't Carlotta. It was a man. I could just see the top of his head and his automobile — a sleek, bright sport car, its top down, its motor running, its radio playing.

One glance in the mirror told me I wouldn't answer the door. I looked a fright. My hair was disheveled, my face puffy from sleep. Anyway, I was hardly dressed to receive a gentleman caller.

I stood at the window and waited. He rang several more times, each time holding his finger on the bell a little longer. Finally he stepped back and looked up. I backed away from the window, but didn't know whether or not I'd been fast enough to escape his notice. I must have been, because he turned and got into his car.

When he looked in my direction I saw his face. He looked a bit like the man who'd driven me to the villa, but this man was younger, slighter of build and even better-looking than Neil — if that was possible. What I really was saying to myself was that this man didn't have an ugly scar on the left side of his face.

The sound of the car's motor drifted into the distance. The quiet was suddenly deafening. I turned from the window and again verified the time. I'd have time for a bath before Carlotta arrived.

★   ★   ★

I was seated at the dressing table putting on the last of my makeup when I heard her car pull into the drive. It skidded to a halt just as I looked down. Carlotta got out from behind the wheel, picked up a huge handbag and started up the stairs onto the terrace. I saw her stop at the potted cypress and fumble around.

The key.

I rushed from the room and down the stairs just as I heard her call my name and bang the large brass door-knocker. I had to smile. Carlotta wasn't the type to trust the subtle sound of an electric buzzer.

I pulled open the door and threw myself into her arms.

'Jen,' she cried. We hugged like two school girls who hadn't seen each other since graduation. 'Oh, Jen,' she said, fighting back the tears. 'You're here at last — and I wasn't here to meet you.'

I held her at arm's length. 'You get younger and prettier with the years,' I said.

'And you just get prettier.' She looked me up and down boldly. 'Yep, you've filled out in all the right places, thank heaven. I was afraid that family of yours would keep you skinny and willowy like the rest of that social set you spin around in.'

She hugged me again and led me

through the foyer into her lair. She slipped her chic light coat over the back of one of the French chairs. She was just as I remembered, short and a bit on the stocky side, yet with an unmistakable air of elegance. Her clothes were expensively cut. She pulled off her wide-brimmed hat and tossed it on the chair with her coat and bag. One would not describe Carlotta as beautiful — she was handsome with bright blue eyes, a regal forehead, a square chin and a flawless creamy complexion.

'I thought Philip might still be here,' she commented.

'He didn't meet me,' I said.

She turned sharply. 'He didn't meet you? Why that no-good louse. But how did you get here? I hope you didn't take one of those infernal taxi cabs? They cheat the life out of you if you aren't familiar with the rates.'

I laughed. 'No, someone by the name of Neil picked me up.'

Carlotta stared at me. Her eyes were wide with what appeared to be shock, or fear. Her eyes moved nervously from side

31

to side. 'Neil? Good lord. I knew I should have stayed and met you myself. Wait until I get my hands on Philip Alenquer.'

'But it's all right, Auntie. Neil was a bit surly, but he got me here in one piece, for which I'm grateful.'

'That isn't the point,' she said. 'Neil Alenquer isn't anyone to trust. He's just not the kind of man I want to have around you.' Her expression was ominous. I'd never seen Carlotta look like this before.

I was innocently confused. I could see no reason for her sudden alarm. 'He seemed a perfect gentleman,' I said. 'He was surly and a bit forceful and silent, but otherwise he seemed harmless enough.'

'Well, he isn't harmless. Just remember that.' She resumed her pacing. Suddenly she stopped, whirled around to face me and put her hands on her hips. 'He's a murderer, that's what he is,' she said.

3

My hand went to my throat. I stared at her.

'Oh, I'm sorry, kid,' she said, turning away from me. 'I shouldn't have said that. It isn't altogether true — at least, nobody could prove anything.'

She came to me and put her arms around me. 'I've upset you. I wish I hadn't. Forget what I said. Come on, let's get you settled. I want to stretch out in a tub then have a couple of stiff belts before dinner. My housekeeper's off for a couple of days so you'll have to put up with my cooking.'

I wasn't listening. All I could think about was that I'd just had a wild ride with a so-called murderer. In spite of the covering up Carlotta was now doing, I couldn't ignore what she'd said. It was horrible. I'd been with a murderer — alone with a murderer.

Carlotta took note of my dismay. 'I didn't mean all that,' she said. She looked embarrassed. 'I sometimes wonder which is worse, my big mouth or my bad temper. No wonder I turned out to be an old maid.'

I shook my head. 'But he seemed so harmless,' I said. 'Who did he kill?'

'Oh, nobody, child. Nobody at all. Neil's wife died and the local gossip is that he was responsible. Of course he wasn't,' she added emphatically. 'There was an investigation and everything, but nothing was ever proven. I didn't mean what I said. Put it out of your mind.'

Carlotta was avoiding my eyes. There was more to her story but I could see I'd have a hard time getting it out of her. She looked most uncomfortable, so for her sake I tried to do what she asked, to push it out of my mind — for the time being.

'I'm not here a day and already excitement is crowding in on me,' I said, smiling. 'Mystery. Intrigue. All I need now is the romance.'

Carlotta smiled too, looking relieved. 'Oh, I've arranged for a bit of romance too. I'm afraid, however, my original plan along that line got off on the wrong foot.'

'That Philip Alenquer fellow? Is he the one you intend throwing at me?'

'Now, I wouldn't throw anybody at anybody. I'll just introduce you, that's all. From that point on you're on your own.'

'Auntie, you know I'm not ready for any of your matchmaking.' I meant it.

She turned and eyed me. 'Still carrying the torch for that Andy Fuller character?'

I couldn't answer. Hearing his name spoken made me think of him — something I tried to avoid.

'He wasn't any good,' she said. 'I told you that when I met him back in the States. He was after your old man's dough and you know it.'

'Please,' I said, 'let's not talk about Andy now. That's over and done with.'

'Is it?'

'Yes.' I picked up my larger suitcase and started toward the stairs. In spite of its weight, it suddenly seemed lighter than my thoughts. Carlotta picked up my other case and followed me.

'Who is the man who called for me at the airport?' I asked as we got to the top of the stairs.

'Neil Alenquer. He's Philip's older brother.'

'Do they live around here?'

She tossed my bag on the bed and nodded in a westerly direction. 'They have the old castle on the next bluff. They're my nearest neighbors. We kind of share this isolation.'

'What do the Alenquers do?'

'Do?' She laughed. 'Now that's a typical American question. Here in Europe when a family lives in a castle and comes from a long line of blue-bloods, they generally do nothing.' She shrugged. 'Oh, I suppose they look after their land holdings, but that's about the extent of it. They're quite well off, although to look at that Neil character one would never suspect it.'

I recalled Neil's attire when he picked me up at the airport. 'Yes,' I said, 'I know what you mean.'

'I bet he looked like an unmade bed. He has always looked like that, ever since . . . ' She let her sentence go unfinished. She turned and started toward a door that I knew connected with her suite of rooms.

'I'm going to soak in a tub. How about getting yourself unpacked? And for heaven's sake, Jen, put on something with a little more flair. That travelling suit looks like you borrowed it from your grandmother.'

'Is it really all that drab?' I asked, eyeing myself in a full-length mirror.

'Drab isn't the word. It makes you look like a doddering old woman. But don't fret, kiddo. We'll change all that with a trip over to Nice or up to Paris. I'll have you looking like a femme fatale in no time at all.'

'But I don't want to be a femme fatale.'

'Every woman wants to be a femme fatale. Even me.'

She went into her rooms but left the door open. I heard her chattering away but couldn't understand any of it.

I started to unpack. I looked at each dress I unfolded as though seeing it for the first time. I had the feeling Carlotta wasn't going to approve. If the truth were known, I had never cared much about fashion and clothes. What I had wanted out of life didn't exist for me anymore.

Andrew Fuller had left me waiting at the altar, so to speak, and he was someone else's now — not mine.

I heard the water being turned on full blast. Carlotta swept back into my room. She was wearing a long lime-green dressing gown. The color was perfect on her. I'd never been able to wear lime-green, not with my dark brown hair and dark eyes. It made me look sallow. Yet it was one of my favorite colors.

'Would you prefer to go out for dinner, Jen?'

I shook out another dress and put it on a hanger. 'No, not really, Auntie.'

'Hey, let's cut out that 'Auntie' stuff. It's okay around your mother and my stuffy brother, but here you'll call me Carlotta, or anything else you like, but definitely not 'Auntie'.' Her eyes fell on the dress I'd unfolded. It was a light beige dinner gown. 'That's nice,' she commented.

Just then the front door buzzer sounded. We looked at each other. Carlotta started toward the window. 'I didn't hear anybody pull up,' she said.

She parted the curtains and looked out and down. 'Philip,' she announced over her shoulder. 'I'll turn off my tub and go down and let him in. Slip into the beige job and come on down.' She was suddenly all aflutter.

I went to the window and peeked out. It was the same man who'd rung the bell when I was sunbathing on the terrace. I had forgotten to mention to Carlotta that he'd been here. I started to shake just a little. I wasn't prepared to meet Philip Alenquer, knowing that Carlotta had purposely planned on throwing us at each other. I truly hated that sort of thing. It always made me more uncomfortable than usual.

'Hurry up,' she said as she came back through my room and out into the hall. The buzzer sounded again.

In spite of my nervousness, I quickly slipped into the dinner gown. As I brushed my hair back and checked my makeup I heard them greeting each other. I stood and studied myself in the mirror for a moment. Then, screwing up my courage, I turned and went downstairs.

They were talking almost in a whisper when I came down. Carlotta heard my steps on the stairs and held up her hand as though cautioning Philip to be quiet.

Philip Alenquer was as good-looking up close as I had thought him to be when I saw him from the window. His hair was dark and curly, but not as unruly or long as Neil's. Yet the similarity between the two men was remarkable. Philip was younger, there was no doubt about that. Twenty-eight, possibly thirty, I decided, but no more. His complexion was dark, his smile contagious. He came directly toward me, holding out both hands.

'So you're Jennifer,' he said, taking my hands in his. He looked me up and down with the boldness I found so common in European men. 'Beautiful. Absolutely beautiful.' He spoke with the same charming accent as his brother.

'This is Philip Alenquer, Jen. How about taking him into the lair and entertaining him until I can get myself together?' She turned to Philip. 'You know where the bar is,' she said. He nodded. 'Fix Jen a martini or something.

She's tired. She could use a pick-me-up; couldn't you, Jen?'

'That might be a little strong for me,' I said. 'I'm afraid I haven't had much to eat except an omelet from your kitchen.'

'You don't have to worry too much about Philip's martinis. They're pure vermouth. They're ghastly things, but one gets used to bad martinis over here.'

Philip laughed. 'I thought you liked my martinis.'

'Let's say I tolerate them,' Carlotta answered with a smile. 'On second thought, how about fixing Philip a real American martini, Jen? Let's show him what a really good martini tastes like. And while you're at it, make a pitcherful. I'm in the mood to celebrate tonight. I got a good commission in Paris today. I'll tell you all about it later.' She hiked up the skirt of her dressing gown and went up the stairs.

'I'll make one of my martinis for you if you'll make one of yours for me,' I told Philip as he headed for the built-in bar at one end of Carlotta's lair.

'Fair enough,' he said. With a sweep of

his hand he added, 'You first. But I warn you, I am not used to strong drinks.'

I hesitated. 'Then perhaps we'd better skip the American martini. It's practically pure gin.'

'No, no. I insist. If you are game to try what we call a martini, I only think it right that I do the same.'

I let Philip produce the glasses and the pitcher. I got a tray of ice from the portable refrigerator.

'Is this your first trip to Europe?' he asked.

I told him it was. I put a few drops of vermouth into the chilled gin, swirled the liquid around, then filled a glass and handed it to him. He sipped it and grimaced.

'Delicious,' he said. He was a charming liar. I grinned.

Then he made a drink for me. I noticed he used no ice. I knew that I wasn't going to like it any more than he had liked the martini I'd made for him. I didn't. It was warm and tasted like pure dry vermouth, as Carlotta had warned me it would. But I didn't complain. I smiled and seated myself on one of the French chairs near the cozy fireplace.

'Would you like a fire?' Philip asked, nodding to the cool black interior of the fireplace.

'Yes, that would be nice, I think. It's gotten cool. Does it always cool down in the evening?'

'Wait until summer. The nights are as warm as the days. You will find yourself longing for some of this coolness.' He started to arrange the logs. He fumbled with some kindling, then struck a match. The fire caught immediately. He knelt back, staring at it. 'A fire makes a room, don't you agree?'

'Yes. There's nothing more cheerful.'

Just then Carlotta swept in. She couldn't have had time to both bathe and dress. Wearing a dinner dress of flowing orange, she almost dimmed the brilliance of the fire by her presence. She looked lovely. I wondered why she had hurried so, but perhaps she didn't want to leave me too long in the company of a man I didn't know.

'How are the drinks coming?' she boomed.

Philip got up. 'Permit me,' he said as he went to the bar with me and picked up the bottle of vermouth.

'Oh, no you don't,' Carlotta said. 'I want one of Jen's martinis. I suddenly feel a little homesick.'

I laughed and started to fix the drink.

'And now,' Carlotta started, settling herself in a chair, addressing herself to Philip, 'I have a bone to pick with you, young man. You left my niece waiting at the airport. Why?'

Philip gave her a blank look and looked at me. 'But I did not know,' he said.

'You got my message,' Carlotta persisted. 'I talked to Theresa myself. I told her I had to go to Paris and I gave her Jen's flight number and time of arrival. I told her to make sure you picked her up.'

'But I received no such message,' he insisted.

'Then how did Neil — ' Carlotta suddenly cut off. She sat there staring at Philip. They were talking with their eyes. I didn't understand their conversation.

Neither spoke for several minutes. Whatever had to be said, suddenly didn't need saying.

4

Philip reached for his drink and downed it in one gulp. I frowned. He had told me he wasn't used to strong cocktails.

'Well, never mind,' Carlotta said brightly. 'You're forgiven. There was a misunderstanding. Perhaps Theresa thought the message was for either you or your brother. It doesn't really matter. Jen's here now; that's all I care about.'

I walked over and handed her the martini I'd made for her.

'Delicious, darling.' She sighed and leaned back in her chair, holding the cocktail poised in front of her. The ragged edge seemed to have been taken off the conversation.

'I've had marvelous things happen for me in Paris,' Carlotta announced. 'Madame Corday wants me to do next year's spring line for them. I couldn't be more pleased. It means quite a bundle for my bank account, to say nothing of the notoriety and prestige.'

'How marvelous,' I enthused. I knew she was purposely changing the subject and I encouraged it.

Philip stared at his empty glass. His mind wasn't on Carlotta's announcement — that was obvious by the look on his face.

'Another drink, Philip?' Carlotta asked.

'What? Oh, no,' he stammered. He pushed the glass away and started to get up. 'I stopped by just to say hello. I should be getting home.' His eyes settled on me and he smiled. 'But I had no idea you had such a lovely house guest. Yes, perhaps I will have another cocktail. But if you do not mind, Jennifer, I believe I will fix my own. As you said, your American martinis are quite strong.'

'And then you can take us into the village for dinner,' Carlotta said. 'I've decided I'm not in the mood to cook tonight. I feel like celebrating a bit.'

'I would be delighted,' Philip said as he fixed himself another drink.

The telephone on the Louis XV desk rang.

I always feel I'm eavesdropping whenever

I'm in the presence of someone engaged in a private telephone conversation. Philip looked as uneasy as I when Carlotta started to speak. She spoke in French, which I couldn't understand, but I could tell by looking at him that Philip did.

He leaned toward me. 'And how do you like Portugal?'

I gave a shrug. 'I've hardly seen any of it, but what I've seen I like very much.'

'I regret the confusion about your aunt's message to me. My brother, Neil, has a tendency to be a little 'rough around the edges' sometimes.'

His use of American slang, spoken with a Portuguese accent, made me laugh. 'He was fine,' I told him.

Our eyes met and held for a moment. The openness with which he looked at me made me flush slightly.

Carlotta was talking rapid French. Then she said, 'Tomorrow? No, impossible.'

Philip and I glanced at her, then at each other.

'Have you lived in Portugal all of your life?' I asked him.

'Yes, except for a year or two. I lived in Paris for a while.'

'It must be exciting to be able to live close to one's home, yet have the opportunity of living with other cultures, other languages. At home, I mean, one can travel hundreds and hundreds of miles, yet wherever you go, unless, say, you live near the Mexican border, everyone speaks the same language. Lifestyles and customs are pretty much the same. Over here, you don't have to travel far before lifestyles, languages and cultures are completely different from your own. It's wonderful exposure.'

'Ah, yes, I see what you mean. That is true,' he said, nodding and smiling.

Carlotta let out a heavy sigh. Whatever battle she was fighting on the phone, it was one she wasn't winning. Finally she dropped the receiver into its cradle. 'Well, you kids might just as well count me out for tonight.' She picked up her cocktail and drained the glass. 'That was Paris. They want some renderings from me by tomorrow. Which means I'll be burning the midnight oil tonight. I'm sorry, Jen. I explained that you'd just arrived this morning, but they insisted.' Carlotta poured herself another martini. She looked annoyed.

'Don't worry about me, Carlotta. I'm a little tired anyway. I'll fix us some dinner while you work.'

'You'll do nothing of the kind. And you can't be all that tired. You slept this afternoon, didn't you?' She glanced at Philip. 'Take Jen someplace nice for dinner.'

'That would please me very much,' he said. He looked almost boyish with his innocent smile, a stray lock of dark hair dangling over his forehead. My heart gave a little thud.

'How about driving into Faro?' Carlotta suggested. 'It's only about an hour's drive. That should keep both of you out of my hair for a while.'

She was already busying herself at the desk. We would only serve as a distraction if we stayed. I got to my feet. 'I'll get a wrap,' I told Philip. As I started out of the lair I stopped in front of Carlotta. 'Are you sure you don't mind?'

'I'm sure,' she mumbled, rummaging through the large case she'd had with her when she returned from Paris.

* * *

The moon was out in all its glory. We drove along the towering bluff and turned inward, away from the sea. 'It is a little shorter over the Serra de Monchique,' he said. 'After we eat we will take the longer coastal route back, if you like.'

'That sounds very nice,' I told him. 'I must admit, I'm a bit famished at present.'

Despite the fact that Philip was more or less a stranger to me, I felt comfortable and relaxed with him. Philip was considerate and easy to talk to. The sleek little sports car bumped and thumped over the somewhat uneven, narrow road to Faro. I felt myself utterly at peace.

'The Serra de Monchique,' Philip said, indicating the purple-hued mountains ahead. 'They are very beautiful, yes?'

'Yes, very.' In the dimness of the night they loomed high and majestic, their crests outlined against the deep blue of the night sky. We came around a sweeping curve and started to climb.

'You have mountains like this in Missigan?'

'Michigan,' I corrected with a smile. 'I'm afraid not, not like this. It's rather flat in Michigan. Just farmlands and lakes. It's very beautiful though.'

'If you come from there, it must be beautiful.'

Again I felt the color rising in my face. 'Are all European men so flattering?'

'Only when flattery is justified.'

My color deepened. I liked Philip Alenquer, not only because he was saying the things I had wanted Andrew Fuller to say. Andy had never said anything complimentary unless he had an ulterior motive. I wondered suddenly if all men were like that. Was Philip Alenquer?

'Are you getting cold? I will stop and put up the top,' he said without waiting for me to answer. He stopped the car on a wide shoulder. We were high up on the mountain. Far below us to the northwest I could discern the graceful coastline with its blinking lights, its shimmering water. A tiny village huddled in the middle of a wide, low expanse of farmland. Looking down from my lofty peak, the town reminded me of home. I thought again of Andrew Fuller and turned my eyes away, shivering. Why had he followed me to Portugal?

Then Philip was back and Andrew Fuller disappeared. 'I was watching you,' Philip admitted when we were underway again. 'You were thinking about the man your aunt told me you came here to forget.'

I frowned slightly and looked down at the floor. 'My aunt talks too much,' I said.

'Your aunt has talked much of you. She is very fond of you.'

My annoyance melted. 'And I of her,' I told him.

'Yes. She is an easy woman to become fond of.' For a while he was lost in his own private thoughts.

We breached the crest of the mountain and the car dipped down. The scene that lay before me was breathtaking.

'The Algarve,' Philip said, again nodding forward. 'It is an Arabic word. It means 'The West'.'

'Oh, Philip,' I enthused. 'How lovely. It's like something from another world, another century.'

'It is another world, another century,' he said. 'The people of the Algarve are aware that there is another world out there beyond the Atlantic horizon, but they have very little interest in it. They feel they have found their Eden and are happy to stay within its boundaries.'

The shoreline stretched, seemingly forever. Seeing the Algarve region, I could understand why Carlotta had said it was the most beautiful place in Portugal, if not in the world.

'But you must come here by day. It is even more beautiful. The moon is jealous of our beautiful region and dims it as best she can.'

We left the crisp air of the mountains, talking all the while of Portuguese history, of the Phoenicians, Carthaginians, Visigoths, Vikings, troops of Napoleon and Wellington — all conquerors of this wonderful land. Philip was not only handsome, poetic and charming; he was intelligent and a fascinating speaker. We crept through sleepy little towns on our way to the shore. The flinty peasants with their swarthy Moorish complexions and the hard-working fishermen remained distinctly Algarvese — not Portuguese, not Moorish or Spanish.

'The distinction is so pronounced,' Philip told me, 'that during the days of the Portuguese monarchy the Algarve province was recognized as a separate kingdom. The king was ruler over Portugal and the Algarve.' He chuckled. 'It is like that even today.'

I glanced at my watch; we had been travelling for over an hour, yet it seemed like minutes. Suddenly we were on the coast and the lovely antiquity of the Algarve was almost obliterated. One had to look hard for traces of the old in the midst of tall new luxury hotels, shimmering glass and steel resorts. It was all so modern and new that it almost depressed me. The change was sudden, drastic and complete.

'The outside world refuses to let the Algarve rest.' Philip drove faster past the modern luxury hotels. It was as if he refused to recognize their existence. I sympathized with him. The glass and steel had no place here. They belonged in a fast progressive world, not the world of crumbling Moorish castles, Roman invaders, and English crusaders.

We didn't drive far before we were again in a quaint little fishing village. 'Faro is a little farther,' Philip explained, pulling the car toward the edge of the street. 'But it is very much like that back there. I am afraid Faro has become very commercial, but I think you will like this taverna. The food is excellent, the wine superb.'

The taverna was a tumbledown cottage tucked in among the charming small shops and houses of the village. 'I hope they won't consider me overdressed,' I said as I swished my long skirt around me and got out of the car.

'They will only stare at you because of your beauty,' he answered with a smile.

The restaurant was no more than a large room with small tables scattered about without pattern or design. Crisp white cloths and carefully polished glasses sparkled under the light of the single candle that adorned each table. The room was lovely. It was also redolent with the most delicious odors.

A dark-haired, dark-complexioned man in an impeccable white apron scurried over to us and bowed. Philip conversed with him in Portuguese. The only word I understood was 'America' when he nodded toward me. The man took my hand, smiled and bowed and mumbled several words. He motioned toward a table isolated a bit from the others, all the while chattering away. Philip was obviously no stranger to the place.

'They have no printed menu here,' Philip told me after we were seated. 'But I am sure you will like the food. It is very good.'

'I'm sure I will,' I told him as the man in the white apron set a carafe of red wine at Philip's elbow.

'Do you like clams?' he asked as he filled my wine glass.

'It's one of my favorite dishes. We eat a lot of them in Michigan.'

He lifted his glass in a toast 'Here is to Michigan for sending you to us.'

The wine was as superb as Philip had said — dark and rich and delicious.

'Too bad Carlotta wasn't able to come with us,' I said.

'If I am to be honest, I must say I do not mind terribly.' He was smiling again, his eyes sparkling with boyish devilment 'And we would not have come here. Carlotta does not like the place. She says it is too provincial. I fear your aunt is a snob.'

I glanced at him quickly but he was smiling still. He didn't mean his remark in the way it sounded. I could tell that by his grin, yet there was something in his eyes that disturbed me.

'A very delightful and lovable snob,' he added as he sampled his wine.

We didn't linger long over the wine before the man was back, this time accompanied by a plump, happy-faced woman bearing a portable table which, between them, they set up next to our table. While we watched, they fussed with lighting a burner and carting in ingredients — plates of various vegetables, meats, clams.

'*Cataplana*,' the woman said, mouthing the word slowly when she spoke to me.

She tested the heat of the copper container, a metal pan shaped like a clam. Obviously satisfied with the temperature, she dropped in a little oil and when it quickly sizzled, added various vegetables and herbs. Finally she dropped in handfuls of freshly dug clams. She slammed down the lid and left us to sip our wine.

We talked about Carlotta, Portugal, Michigan. We did not talk about Neil. The smells coming from the copper pan were excruciatingly delicious.

I suppose it was my hunger that made me drink more wine than usual. And I blamed the wine for my boldness in saying, 'You're so very different from your brother, Neil.'

For a split second I saw something in his face that I would have preferred not to identify. Then his expression softened. He gave a helpless little gesture. 'Neil is a strange man. But — he has had a very unhappy time of it. It is no wonder he is bitter and disillusioned.'

'Why do you say that?' I asked. But if I were to have my curiosity satisfied, I found it would have to be by someone other than Philip.

'Neil has always been the unfortunate one. Tragedy follows him like a shadow.' He shook his head. 'Poor man; he is to be pitied.'

'Having met him, I would say pity is not what he would welcome.'

'He is a very proud man. Too proud. He has always been too proud. But perhaps it is just as well. It is a defense he can hide behind. You will most likely see him again during your visit, so perhaps I had best explain,' Philip said.

I felt suddenly tense, and made no reply.

'Neil was not always so serious, so unhappy. It began when we were very small. You see, my parents were burned to death when their yacht caught fire and sank. Neil and I were aboard the yacht, but luckily we escaped harm. Unfortunately, my father's and mother's death weighed heavily on Neil. More heavily on Neil than on me, for some reason or

other. The accident left Neil a bit
. . . strange.'

'How horrible,' I breathed. Unconsciously I reached for my wine glass and
sipped.

Philip sighed and toyed with the stem
of his glass. He sat swirling the red liquid
around inside its bowl. His thoughts were
far, far away. I wasn't certain he was
going to talk about Neil's later problems.

'Is that how he got his scar?' I asked
hesitantly.

'No.'

The cook was back, chattering away.
She babbled something to Philip, put
plates down in front of us and flipped
open the lid of the *cataplana*. Steam,
heavy with the smells of fresh vegetables
and herbs and newly opened shellfish,
rose in a cloud. The combination of
vegetables and clams, I found, tasted as
good as the smell — a wonderful blend of
the best flavors of sea and earth.

Neil was pushed into the background.
The rest of the evening was spent
relishing the food, the wine, and the
freshly baked bread smeared with creamy

butter straight from the churn. It was a simple, yet handsome meal.

I felt content with everything and everyone when I pushed my plate away and finished my wine. 'How absolutely delicious,' I announced. 'I'm afraid I made a glutton of myself.'

Philip winked. 'They expect that of you here.'

After another short session of bows and smiles, we found ourselves outside under the dark, warm sky of the Algarve. The night was even more beautiful than before. The moon didn't seem jealous of the region now; she shined brightly, illuminating every corner, every shadow.

'Your aunt would appreciate our staying out a bit longer,' Philip said. 'Are you too tired to do some moonlight touring?'

'No, I feel marvelous. I'm not the least bit tired now. I guess I'm running on nervous energy. I'll collapse tomorrow.'

He laughed. 'Good. There are many lovely places to see.'

He started up the car. We turned up a hill and drove along the coast for a few miles. At the hillside town of Silves, Philip insisted I see an old sandstone castle which the Moors had left standing as a reminder of their powerful presence and of the time when the crusaders had stopped off to sack the town on their way to the holy land.

From Silves we went back down toward the walled seaport of Lagos with its medieval casbah and its handsome, shimmering bay. History crowded in on every side. I remembered things which I thought I had buried with my history books. I remembered the one-armed admiral sailing by for a rendezvous at Cape Trafalgar, Prince Henry the Navigator who watched the caravels of Vasco da Gama and his other explorers sail off to adventure and discovery.

Later, we stood high on the seawall looking out over the placid beauty of the water with its gleaming ribbon of moonbeam. Philip was close; I could feel his hip touching mine. I was overly conscious of his nearness. Then all thoughts of history were suddenly shoved from my mind as Philip's arm went around my waist. I felt it tighten. He turned me gently.

'You are so very lovely,' he said softly. He pulled me hard against him.

'No, Philip, please,' I said, easing myself out of his embrace.

'You do not like me?' he asked as I turned from him.

I didn't answer. I couldn't. How could I tell him that it was just the opposite — that I liked him too much? — and that I knew I was too vulnerable.

5

From what I could see out my bedroom
window, it was a bright, glorious morning
— a perfect morning for a stroll along the
beach. I took a stinging cold shower,
trying to wash away my drowsiness. My
body felt tired, yet my mind was wide
awake.

Carlotta was sound asleep when I
peeked in on her. I slipped into a
swimsuit, threw a terrycloth robe over my
shoulders and trotted downstairs to the
kitchen. While I fixed myself some
breakfast I thought about Philip Alenquer. I had to smile at my weak excuse,
telling him that girls didn't usually kiss on
a first date in America. I had wanted him
to kiss me. And he could have.

But Philip was a gentleman. He kissed
my hand when we drove up in front of
Carlotta's villa. He said he would see me
again soon, perhaps today if his schedule
permitted. And then he took his leave,

waiting to make certain I was safely inside before driving away.

'Nice,' I said aloud, conjuring up Philip's face in my mind's eye.

'What's nice?' Carlotta asked, yawning and rubbing her hand over the back of her neck. She was wearing the same lime-green dressing gown I'd seen her in last night. Her hair was disheveled, her eyes puffy. She looked older than I had imagined. 'I know, I know. I look a fright.' She shuffled over to the stove and poured herself a cup of coffee. 'Ugh. This is awful. I'll have to show you how to make coffee, I see.' She threw the whole potful into the sink and started from scratch. I saw that I'd added too much coffee. And Carlotta used bottled water, not the water from the tap, as I had.

'What time did you get in last night?' she asked.

'A little after midnight. The light in the lair was on, but I didn't want to disturb you.'

Carlotta merely grunted. 'Well, I finished the renderings. Paris said their messenger would be here to pick them up at noon. What time is it now?'

I wasn't wearing my watch. 'About eleven,' I told her. 'Why don't you go back to bed? I can wait for the messenger.'

'No, I'm up now. I'll nap later this afternoon.'

'I was thinking of a dip in the ocean.'

'A dip in the Atlantic, my dear child, is for the very young or the very foolish. All that salt water. It's bad for the skin. How was last night? Did Philip try anything?'

'What do you mean?'

'Oh, come, come, Jen. Did he try to make love to you?'

'He tried, but he didn't get very far.'

'Why not?'

'I consider myself to be a nice girl.'

She dismissed my remark with a wave of her hand. 'Too bad.'

I threw back my head and laughed. 'You're impossible.'

'He's a good catch. I think you might get him if you play your cards right.'

I gave her an admonishing look. 'I am not looking for a good catch. I didn't come over here to find myself a husband.

Just a vacation, and some peace of mind.'

'There's plenty of time ahead of you for peace of mind and vacations,' she said. 'You aren't getting any younger, kiddo. Don't be like me and wait until it's too late.'

'That wasn't because you didn't have the chance, I bet.'

Her eyes got misty. 'Oh, I had plenty of chances. I just fell in love with the wrong guy, that's all.'

'A married man?' I asked.

'No, just not available. How's that coffee coming along?'

I knew immediately that the subject, brief as it was, was closed. She wouldn't talk of it anymore, and I didn't feel I should press her, although I wanted to. Carlotta in love? I wondered idly what kind of man he'd been.

The sun was streaming in through the windows. Thoughts of romance made me think of Philip. I suddenly wanted to be alone. 'I'm going down to the beach. I'll see you later.'

'Maybe I'll come down and join you in a little while.'

'Fine. I'd like that.'

I picked up my robe and went out into the blazing sun. Just as I stepped onto the terrace I heard the doorbell ring. I hesitated. Perhaps it was Philip. I waited, listening. Suddenly I felt foolish standing there like a schoolgirl waiting for her date. It was more than likely the messenger from Paris — early.

I went across the terrace and down the long flight of wooden stairs. They were old and rough. I took my time on the way down, using the poor condition of the steps as an excuse. Actually I was waiting to hear Carlotta call me to tell me Philip was there. She didn't. A gull swooped and called a greeting before it zoomed back into the sky, circled and swooped down toward me again.

On stepping into the crashing surf I found it was much too cold for swimming. I decided I'd lie in the sun, but I'd forgotten a towel. *Besides*, I told myself, *you're too keyed up to laze on a beach. Go for a walk. Keep active.*

Whether my direction was taken on purpose or purely subconsciously I really can't say, but after a long, long walk around the curve of the bay I came upon a large sign. 'Trespassers Will Be Prosecuted,' I translated, relying on my high school French. The sign bore the name 'N. Alenquer.'

But surely the sign was intended for strangers. I certainly could not be considered a trespasser. Carlotta was friends with the Alenquers, and besides, there would be no harm in thanking Philip for last night. So I ducked under the heavy chain that stretched across the sand, anchoring itself to a large iron post some distance out in the surf, barely visible in the churning foam.

Their beach, like Carlotta's, was completely deserted. But unlike Carlotta's, from the looks of things I could readily see that it was seldom, if ever, used. Driftwood lay everywhere and fly-infested seaweed lay in hulking masses, spotting the waterline most unattractively.

I walked slowly, picking my way through the debris, careful not to cut my unprotected feet on the sharp jagged edges of the various shells that had been washed up on the sand. As I came in sight of the Alenquer castle, nestled at the edge of the high bluff, I couldn't help but feel a sense of anxious foreboding.

'Ouch,' I gasped as my foot connected with a pointed fragment of shell. I hobbled on one foot, brushing the other with my hand, unable to see if any real damage had been done. Cold water or not, I decided I'd best wash off my foot in the surf.

A large seashell lay at the edge of the water, rocking back and forth in the fast-moving tide. I stopped to inspect my find. I knew absolutely nothing about shells, and if anyone had told me what it was I doubt very much if I would have remembered. Still, it was a magnificent thing, multicolored and sparkling brilliantly in the morning sun.

I set my treasure between my legs and seated myself on the warm, soft sand. The water felt icy as it lapped at my feet and ankles, but the hurt feeling at the bottom of my foot soon vanished as a result of the water's soothing massage.

I leaned back, digging my elbows into

the moist softness of the beach, and stared up at the blue cloudless sky overhead. The sun burned into my eyes. I squinted at a raft a short distance out, bobbing and lolling in rhythm with the shifting waves. Suddenly I was tempted to swim out to it. I'd swum in colder water than this back home, I reminded myself. I stood, dropping my robe a safe distance from the lapping water's edge.

I had taken three or four steps out into the surf when suddenly I spun around as the blunt crack of what sounded like a rifle shot broke the stillness of the morning. Fractions of a second later, a bullet slashed the water, inches from my legs.

I stared, bewildered, searching the direction from which the shot had come. I was puzzled and more annoyed than frightened. I never considered for a moment that someone had picked me as a target for their rifle practice. I stood frozen to the spot, gaping up at the sharp rise of tangled brush that rambled upward to meet the castle's distant terrace.

A second rifle shot raised my temper to boiling. The bullet sprayed the sand only inches in front of me and, alarmed now, I fell into the surf. I struggled to my feet, splashing the water with the palms of my hands, lumbering forward, gasping, sputtering, trying to escape the out-rushing current that tried to tug me off balance. My hair hung over my face. My mouth tasted of salt. I coughed and choked as I fought my way to the beach.

Again the rifle cracked. I flew across the short span of beach, heedless of the sharp pebbles that dug at my bare feet. The bullet spewed up sand just to the right of me. Suddenly I was scared. My body began to tremble. Whoever was shooting was not merely practicing; their aim was too deliberate. They were shooting at me.

I threw myself flat on the sand and crouched as low as possible behind a tangle of driftwood. I held my breath, waiting for the rifle fire. I stayed there for what seemed hours. Nothing happened.

I peeked out from behind my barricade and looked up. He was standing high above, at his hip a rifle pointed in my direction. The sun was on him. Neil Alenquer looked more menacing, more frightening than ever. There was no doubt it was Neil. The hair was shaggier than Philip's, the body taller, heavier. He was wearing the same formless trousers and heavy boots he had worn yesterday.

The moment I saw him turn away I bolted. I forgot about my robe, my bruised feet. I ran as fast as I could until I reached the chain and its threatening sign. I scooted under and raced along the beach until my legs finally gave out from under me and I collapsed in a heap. I started to cry.

How long I stayed there, crying from fright, I can't be certain. It was Carlotta's voice that roused me. I heard her calling my name.

The sound of her voice brought me to my senses. I couldn't have her find me like that. Quickly I sat up, brushing the tears from my cheeks. I rubbed my eyes with the backs of my hands. I thought suddenly about the robe I'd left lying on the Alenquer beach. I hoped Carlotta wouldn't notice its absence.

I suddenly remembered Carlotta's reaction yesterday to the mention of Neil Alenquer's name. She'd be furious if I told her what had happened. I couldn't start trouble between them. And I had been responsible, in a way. It was I who had ignored the 'No Trespassing' sign. I had wandered onto property where I was not welcome and did not belong.

Carlotta came round the curve of the beach, trudging toward me. I made up my mind I would not tell her what had happened. After all, no harm had befallen me. Neil had just tried to scare me, that was all.

'Didn't you bring a towel down with you? I thought I saw you with one,' she said, noticing its absence.

I didn't look at her. 'No, I forgot a towel.' I didn't mention the robe and Carlotta didn't ask, so she must not have remembered my having one with me.

'What are you doing way down here? You're almost to the Alenquer beach.'

'Oh, am I?'

'It's just around the bend. Thank

74

goodness you didn't go over there. Neil guards the place like it was Fort Knox.'

'Why?'

Carlotta flopped down onto the sand beside me, not caring about the sun dress she was wearing. 'There are a lot of tourists who know about the death of his wife. They come around now and then just to gawk.'

'I see,' I said. 'It must be terrible for him. When did his wife die?'

'A long time ago. Ten years, maybe.'

I looked up sharply. 'That long ago? Surely people don't still come around to gawk at him?'

'You don't know people, honey. Some folks just never forget a scandal.'

'He must have loved his wife very much.'

'Yes, I suppose he did. Maybe he loved her too much. Some people do, you know.'

'Love too much? Yes, I know.'

We sat there, neither of us speaking for a while, each wrapped up in her own personal memories. Then Carlotta slapped her hands on her thighs and started to push herself up. 'Come on, Jen. I want to take you into Lisboa this afternoon for some shopping. It's a nice long drive, so we'd better get started.'

'I thought you were going to lie down this afternoon.'

'No, I'm not tired anymore. A drive into the city will do me good. I've been cooped up with business too much lately. I want to spend a little money and have a bit of fun. Come on.'

'Isn't that the same drive I came over yesterday from the airport?'

Carlotta laughed. 'Yes, but I bet any amount of money you didn't see much of it with Neil behind the wheel.'

I had to smile. 'You'd win,' I told her, getting to my feet. I was immediately reminded of the cuts on the soles of my feet. I tried to ignore them but I couldn't ignore the shaking of my knees, the weakness in my legs. A man had shot at me. I shivered.

'Cold? You should have brought along a robe.'

6

I changed into a light print dress for our shopping trip, and dabbed some medication on my cut feet. I had a strange sense of foreboding. Surely Neil hadn't meant me any harm; he was only trying to frighten me. I was certain he was no criminal. He'd had every opportunity to do me bodily harm on the way from the airport, but he hadn't. He'd been gruff and a bit ill-mannered, but that didn't mean he was a criminal. And why had he come to pick me up, anyway?

Neil was a bit strange, that was true, but from the little I had seen of him I had gotten the feeling of honesty and trust. Maybe, being the older of the two sons, he felt responsible for the deaths of his parents. He couldn't have been more than in his early teens when the accident had occurred. At that time of life such a catastrophe could very easily leave an indelible scar. He hadn't gotten his facial scar then, though. Had that happened when his wife died? No wonder Neil feared people. It seemed that tragedy met him at every turn.

'Are you almost ready, Jen?' Carlotta called as she came through the connecting door into my room.

I shoved my feet into low-heeled shoes and pretended they didn't hurt. 'Ready,' I told her as I came out of the bathroom. I hurriedly pushed Neil into the background. 'Do I look all right?' I stood there waiting for an opinion on my summer print.

Carlotta gave me a cursory glance. 'You'll blend in well with all the rest of the tourists,' she said with a faint smile on her lips.

'Is it that bad?'

'Only when you're dealing with tradespeople. They raise the prices for tourists.'

'That doesn't sound like a very fair practice.'

'Perhaps not, but unfortunately it's a universal practice. Come on, let's go before it gets any later. Most of the shops close up during the heat of the afternoon but some of the bigger ones stay open for the benefit of the tourist traffic.'

As I walked beside her down the stairs and out of the villa I was thankful for her chatter. It took my mind off the problem of deciding whether I should tell her about the shooting incident which weighed so heavily on my mind. I felt I was being a traitor to Carlotta by not telling her.

Just as we started down the drive in Carlotta's car, Philip's sleek little sport car turned in through the gates and started toward us. He honked the horn and waved. He looked so fresh, so alive in his open-necked white shirt and jaunty scarf — so European, I thought as I smiled at him.

'And where are you two lovely ladies off to?'

'Lisboa,' Carlotta told him. 'Shopping.'

'I wish I could come along,' Philip said. His eyes were fixed firmly on mine.

'I'm glad you can't,' Carlotta said. 'We're going on women's business. We don't want any males hovering in the background.'

Philip laughed, but his gaze never left me. 'You are looking lovely today, Miss Carter.'

'Thank you, kind sir.'

Carlotta eased her foot off the brake. 'We've got to be going, Philip.' I thought I noticed an edge in her voice.

For the first time Philip's eyes wandered from me to Carlotta. 'I just stopped by to see if you ladies would like to have dinner at our place this evening.' His eyes returned to me. 'Theresa, our housekeeper, is an excellent cook. Carlotta will vouch for that.'

Carlotta said nothing. She was hesitating, thinking. I thought it was a marvelous idea, but the look on Carlotta's face told me to remain silent.

'I was thinking we would stay in Lisboa for dinner,' Carlotta said.

Philip looked disappointed. 'I just thought Jennifer would like to see what the inside of a sixteenth-century castle really looks like.'

'Oh, I would,' I said before realizing it.

Carlotta instantly looked defeated. 'Very well. We'll be back around six-thirty.'

'Good. I will pick you up at eight o'clock.' He smiled at me. 'You will become accustomed to late hours after living here for a while. Once the summer weather settles in you will want to sleep the afternoon away. Everyone does. Even the shops close to escape the heat of the day.'

'Yes, so Carlotta said.'

Carlotta looked impatient to be away. 'Eight o'clock then,' she said curtly. The car started away. Philip waved again and was gone.

Carlotta's mood was noticeably changed. She said little on the drive to Lisbon and the only shopping we did was a dress for me — a lovely, thin, flowing affair in a beautiful burgundy. I would not have chosen it for myself, but Carlotta's trained eye insisted I try it on. As in almost everything else, Carlotta's taste proved impeccable. The gown was simply cut; its lines flattered my figure, and its color complemented my hair and my complexion. Thankfully it needed no alterations, as I wanted to wear it to the Alenquer Castle that evening.

'You're unusually quiet this afternoon, Carlotta,' I remarked as we left the shop, box in hand. 'How about showing me some of Lisbon?'

'Another time,' she said. 'We'll have to hurry if Philip is calling for us at eight.' Her features were hard and sharp.

'But it's only five,' I commented, glancing at my watch.

'It's a long drive back.'

'Not that long.'

Then Carlotta's features softened. She sighed and slipped her arm around my waist. She hugged me to her. 'I'm sorry, honey. I'm being somewhat of a drag this afternoon. I guess I'm being selfish.'

'About what?'

'You. I thought you and I would just go off by ourselves. Just the two of us. I suppose I'm a little jealous of Philip's attention. I didn't figure on his falling for you like a ton of bricks.'

My color suddenly deepened. 'You're exaggerating.'

'Oh, no I'm not. I know Philip pretty well. He's an open book to me.'

I followed Carlotta's example and slipped my arm around her waist. We sauntered along, hip to hip. 'I came here to be with you, not Philip Alenquer. We don't have to go there for dinner tonight if you don't want to. Let's call and say we've changed our minds. It's a woman's prerogative, you know.'

Carlotta laughed and I felt better. 'No. We'll go. Philip's right. You should see what the inside of a castle is like, especially one that is lived in. These tourist attractions are always so cold and unfriendly; you can never get the feel of what those old stone barns were like when they were actually inhabited. And the Alenquer place dates back to about 1590, after King Philip II seized the Portuguese throne. Philip's great-great-grandmother was a daughter of King Philip, an honest-to-God princess.' She paused. 'Of course, today Portugal is what they call a corporate republic, so royalty doesn't have much of an advantage — except socially, of course.'

We were strolling along the Avenida da Liberdade with its patterned mosaic sidewalks in muted pastels. Tree-sheltered cafés lined both sides of the avenue, and behind their tables and chairs the buildings were high and old and packed together. The street was wide, and at various intersections huge marble statues beckoned or frowned or stared in silence at the cars and pedestrians as they passed. Carlotta motioned toward an empty table at one of the sidewalk cafés, and we sat there.

'Will Neil be there tonight?' I asked hesitantly.

'I suppose so,' she said. 'He does live there, you know. Why?'

'I was just wondering.'

She reached across the small table to touch the back of my hand. 'Look, try to forget my slip the other day. Neil's a good enough sort. He's just a bit strange.'

I had to laugh. 'That's exactly the way Philip described him.'

'He spoke to you about Neil?' Her eyes were wide with surprise.

The waiter sauntered over. Carlotta said something in Portuguese. He bowed and departed.

'He only told me about how their parents died. Horrible,' I said, shaking my head.

'He didn't mention Neil's wife?'

'No, he didn't. How did she die?'

'In a fire.' Carlotta fumbled with the gloves and bag in her lap.

'How awful. And what a ghastly coincidence, their parents dying in a fire also. Is that why people suspected Neil when his wife died?'

'Something like that. Oh, here comes the waiter. I think you'll like this aperitif. It's a Madeira, a dry one called Sercial. It tastes like champagne, don't you think?'

I sipped and nodded. She was obviously changing the subject again.

'We'll come back to Lisboa often while you're here,' Carlotta said. 'It's a charming city, one of the most beautiful in the world.'

'Yes, it is lovely here,' I said, relaxing back in my chair.

'And there's so much to see — and buy. You'll have to act as my chaperone when it comes to spending money, Jen. I'm afraid my shopping sprees are few and far between, but once I get started there's no stopping me.' She tossed down her Sercial and started collecting herself. 'We'd best get started back. I'll show you some of the countryside this time. And I promise I won't be so glum.'

We had a leisurely drive back along the

coast and through the cork forests of Baixo Alentejo, the low province beyond the Tagus River. On one side was the ocean in all its majestic beauty. On the other side, here and there, rice fields gave way to hillsides dotted with clumps of dark red houses and heavy green-smelling pine. We stopped at Setubal, where Carlotta bought a box of orange cakes that she said Philip simply adored. I tasted one; it was overly sweet, chewy and smelled of orange oil from the peel. I grimaced and offered the uneaten piece to Carlotta. She shook her head.

'I wouldn't dare. My figure, you know.' Her laugh had a haunted quality to it. She was merely pretending for my sake.

We arrived back at the villa a little before seven. The sky was much darker and the moon was high and full. Carlotta stood and stared up at it for a moment.

'What's wrong?' I asked.

She shook herself. 'Nothing. Come along. Philip will be here in an hour.'

Philip arrived in less than an hour. I was just putting the finishing touch to my makeup and Carlotta was brushing her hair when the front doorbell sounded.

'I had a feeling he'd be a little early,' she called to me through the open connecting door. 'Can you go down and let him in, Jen?'

The folds of the wine-colored dinner gown moved gracefully about me as I ran downstairs and opened the door.

Philip couldn't have looked more handsome. His white dinner jacket accented his black hair and olive complexion. His eyes were soft and sparkling when he smiled at me. 'Ravishing,' he breathed. He reached for me. I stepped back and extended my hand. There was an impish smile on my lips. 'I am slightly early,' he said as he stepped into the foyer. 'I hope I am not inconveniencing you.'

'No, we're both ready,' Carlotta called as she started down the stairway. Philip looked up at her.

He had a right to stare. I had never seen Carlotta look so beautiful. She was dressed in a simple white gown with a diamond necklace at her throat. She wore no other adornment. She looked very young and very beautiful.

Philip had driven the limousine. It had been recently washed and polished, and its interior carefully vacuumed. He held the door open for us; Carlotta and I got into the back seat and Philip got behind the wheel. Within five minutes we were entering the grounds of Alenquer Castle. They were, I was dismayed to see, in a terrible state of neglect.

At first I didn't see the castle; the trees were so tall and thick, the undergrowth dense and untended. Leaves cluttered the drive as we swept up the long, winding road. We came to a clearing.

Alenquer Castle perched proudly on a knoll, overlooking the ocean. It was a huge, dark, rambling affair with multiple turrets and towers. Grinning stone gargoyles poked out from cornices and crevices. The windows were massive leaded arches laced by narrow ribbons of stone.

'It's magnificent,' I said.

'It is Manueline, architecturally speaking,' Philip explained. 'Although it was built by one of my ancestors, it was copied from the style of architecture introduced by King Manuel. It is a bit out of fashion today, but we like it.'

'Oh, so do I,' I said. 'It's breathtaking.'

'Especially by the light of the full moon, yes?'

I thought I heard Carlotta give a little gasp. Philip must have heard it too because I saw him glance at Carlotta in the rear-view mirror.

Neil was standing under the portico when the car drove up. He reached out and opened the door on Carlotta's side. 'Good evening, Carlotta,' he said. I saw her extend her hand. He kissed the back of it. Neil reached to help me out. Our eyes met. He was holding his head erect. The scar on the left side of his face seemed illuminated by the light of the moon. It was indeed an ugly thing, yet I found I could look at it now without flinching. It didn't seem half as grotesque as when I'd first seen it. Perhaps it was because there was a trace of a smile on Neil's lips that helped soften the effects of the disfigurement.

My hand was shaking when he bowed over it. 'Miss Carter,' he said, 'it is an honor to have you here.' His speech sounded rehearsed. He didn't seem any happier about this dinner party than Carlotta.

'Hello, Neil,' I said, trying to sound bright and flippant. 'It's nice to see you again.'

'Shall we go in?' he said, moving toward the door.

If there were any trace of regret for having shot at me that morning, I couldn't detect it. He was calm and cool and exceedingly polite and affable. Perhaps he did not know at whom he had fired his rifle. I had been slightly unnerved at the thought of meeting Neil again so soon after our encounter on the beach; but now, seeing his relaxed manner, I felt calmer.

Philip came up behind me and took my arm, slipping it through his. When we passed Neil I thought I saw the brothers exchange cold looks.

If the exterior of Alenquer Castle was breathtaking, the interior was even more so. It was huge — larger than anything I'd ever seen. A giant marble staircase formed a perfect horseshoe. It ran up one wall, across the top, and down the other wall. It was carpeted in deep burgundy and the walls were covered in stretched cream silk. A massive chandelier, lighted with hundreds of tiny bulbs rather than candles, dominated the entrance hall. In the center of the hall, sitting regally on the gold-veined marble floor, was a heavy round table of Spanish or Portuguese origin which held a display of gladioli.

'Most of the rooms are closed up,' Philip told me. 'It's impossible to maintain them all. We will have our drinks in the salon. It is this way.'

'Quite a layout, don't you think, Jen?' Carlotta said.

'Layout?' Neil asked but Carlotta only laughed and didn't bother to explain.

'It's simply enchanting,' I said, looking around.

Philip shrugged. 'It is home.'

Neil, I noticed, took a seat a little away from the rest of us. He sat in a shadow. If it were not for the stark white of his dinner jacket he would have been almost invisible.

Philip asked about our afternoon in Lisbon.

'Oh, dear,' Carlotta groaned. 'I purposely

stopped at Setubal and picked up some of those orange cakes you like so much, but I left them at the villa.'

Philip took up her hand and pressed it to his lips. He lingered over the kiss. 'Your thoughtfulness is nonetheless appreciated,' he said.

Out of the corner of my eye I could see Neil's eyes watching them. I could not see his face but I felt that his expression was one of disapproval.

'Neil,' Philip called, 'how about fixing the ladies some cocktails? You are much more adept at it than I, and you know the secret of the American martini.'

Neil didn't move for a moment. He merely sat there, slumped in his chair. Finally he pushed himself up and without a word went to a long refectory table where there were dozens of bottles, glasses, and a bowl of ice cubes. 'Do you drink martinis, Miss Carter?' he asked over his shoulder. He sounded as though he disapproved.

'Yes,' I answered him. 'But please call me Jennifer, or Jen if you prefer.'

He busied himself with sloshing liquor

into a pitcher of ice cubes, then adding a dash of dry vermouth. He swirled it around, picked up two glasses and set them before Carlotta and me. 'Olive or lemon peel?' he asked.

'Neither,' I told him. Carlotta also waved away the offer of a garnish.

'You can fix me a Scotch,' Philip said.

Neil gave him a frosty look, but he poured two drinks. He handed one to Philip and retired again to his seat.

Carlotta began chattering about her Paris business — styles, money, people. It seemed she and Philip knew many of the same people in Paris. I remembered that Philip had lived in Paris for a time. I didn't mind Philip paying so much attention to Carlotta, but his attention seemed forced. As they talked, I glanced over at Neil. He was watching them. He must have sensed my eyes on him. He looked at me. I smiled.

'I understand you are from Michigan, Miss Carter.' He was purposely refusing my friendship; I could tell by the way he stressed 'Miss Carter'.

'Yes. Have you ever been there?'

'No. I am afraid I haven't traveled much.'

I fidgeted, trying to think of something to say. All I could think about was his shooting at me. I wondered if he were thinking about the same thing. Philip and Carlotta were wrapped up in gossip about mutual friends and acquaintances. 'It's a very lovely state,' I told Neil. 'I think you'd like it.'

'I suppose I would,' he said indifferently. His eyes were fixed firmly on mine. His look made me squirm uncomfortably, but there was a softness in his eyes. He leaned forward and spoke very softly, almost in a whisper. 'I have something that belongs to you,' he said.

My head turned sharply to see whether Carlotta or Philip had heard him. I was sure they hadn't. They were going on about a certain Monsieur du Val, whoever he was. I looked back at Neil and started to ask him if he was referring to my beach robe, but he held two fingers to his lips and leaned back into the shadow.

When I picked up my glass to sip at the martini, my hand was shaking so badly a few drops splashed down over my dress.

Philip noticed. 'Oh, Jen. Your beautiful dress.' He immediately produced a handkerchief and handed it to me.

'It's nothing,' I said, putting my glass down on the table and taking the handkerchief. 'I'm sure it won't leave a stain.'

Carlotta reached and took my hand. 'Come along. We'll put some cold water on it right away, just in case.' I allowed myself to be led from the salon into a small guest bathroom.

'Well, what did Neil say to you?' Carlotta asked harshly the moment the door closed behind us. She snatched Philip's handkerchief from my hand and began dabbing at the wet spots on my dress. 'I heard him whisper something. What was it?'

'You don't miss a trick, do you?' I asked lightly.

'Not many. Well, what did he whisper?'

'He said he had something that belongs to me.'

'Belongs to you? What? Did you leave anything in the car when he drove you to the villa? Perhaps you dropped something and didn't know it.'

'Perhaps.' I felt terrible. I wasn't lying to Carlotta but I was letting her jump to wrong conclusions and it bothered me immensely.

'There,' Carlotta announced, stepping back and admiring her handiwork. 'The spots are all gone. Come on, let's go back and finish our drinks. I'm famished, aren't you?'

We were no sooner back in the salon when Carlotta asked Neil, 'What do you have of Jennifer's?'

Very slowly a thin trace of a smile appeared at his mouth. I was standing slightly behind Carlotta. Neil's eyes moved briefly to mine. I shook my head sharply.

'A handkerchief,' he said. I thought I saw him glance briefly at Philip's handkerchief, which Carlotta was still holding. 'I will get it. Your niece dropped it in the back seat of the car.'

He got to his feet and walked out of the room. His stride was masculine and purposeful; there wasn't the slightest hesitancy.

'Neil mentioned your near accident,' Philip said after his brother had left the room.

Carlotta whirled on me. 'You said nothing about an accident.'

'It was nothing.' I resumed my seat by the fire and picked up my martini. 'A car cut in front of us. Neil had to swerve to avoid hitting it. I tumbled to the floor along with my luggage. No one was hurt. It wasn't anything serious. I didn't think it worth mentioning.'

'Neil is an impossible driver,' Carlotta said.

A short, heavyset woman in a powder-blue dress and white apron appeared in the doorway. She nodded to Philip.

'Theresa says dinner is ready to be served. Shall we go in?'

I took another sip of my martini. Neil came back into the room. 'Here it is,' he said, handing me a beautiful lace handkerchief.

It wasn't mine. I'd never seen it before. I looked up at him. His eyes were smiling; his lips were not.

'Thank you,' I said, taking the handkerchief and tucking it into the sleeve of my dress.

'That looks familiar,' Carlotta said. She

boldly pulled out the handkerchief and began examining it. 'I have a feeling I've seen this somewhere before.'

Neil took it out of her hand and handed it back to me. Carlotta eyed him suspiciously but said nothing more. She shrugged and took Philip's arm. 'I'm starving,' she said.

Philip gave me a helpless little look. Neil offered me his arm. We went in to dinner. Walking with Neil behind the others, I felt like a conspirator.

The dinner was as magnificent as the room in which it was served. The main course, Philip told me, was *cabrito*, a whole roast kid garnished with slices of orange and sprigs of fresh mint. It was heavenly, although I found myself still a bit uneasy as a result of the episode about the handkerchief. I was overly conscious of it tucked in my long sleeve.

Conversation was polite and casual. Neil said very little. From time to time I caught him staring at me most peculiarly. His stare made me nervous, and being nervous I talked more than usual.

For dessert Theresa served *lampreia*

de ovos, an egg-yolk confection. It was exceptionally delicious, although a bit sweet for my taste.

'I think it is warm enough to have our coffee on the terrace,' Philip said.

As we rose I noticed that Neil continued to sit, oblivious to our conversation, seemingly hypnotized by the flickering flames of the candles.

'Neil,' Philip said sharply.

Neil instantly jumped to his feet and helped me out of my chair. The brothers exchanged looks again.

'It's cold on the terrace,' Neil said. 'The ladies will need wraps. They will be much more comfortable in the salon.' So he hadn't been oblivious to the conversation, I told myself.

'Nonsense,' Carlotta boomed. 'A little fresh air is good for us.' She linked her arm with Philip's and started out through the massive French doors that led to the terrace overlooking the sea.

The moon was out in all its full, round glory. The path of light it trailed across the ocean shimmered and bobbed with the rolling tide. The terrace, wider and longer than Carlotta's, was lighted by torches that blazed brightly and threw an eerie, macabre light. Comfortable chairs were scattered about. We settled ourselves, although I found myself agreeing with Neil; it was more than just a bit chilly.

I leaned back in my chair, snuggling against the cushions for warmth. Everyone seemed to be relaxing after the wonderful meal. No one said anything for a while.

My thoughts wandered back to another moon, another time, another place — a summer house on Lake Michigan. I stared up at the moon, thinking again about Andrew. He had proposed by the light of a full moon and quoted a poem of Shelley's. Without realizing I was speaking aloud, I said, ''That orbed maiden with white fire laden, whom mortals call the moon'.'

Theresa suddenly dropped the tray of coffee things she was carrying out. Neil jumped to his feet. Philip turned and stared. Carlotta gasped. Her hand went to her throat as she stared at me.

I sat bolt upright. 'What is it?' I stammered. 'What did I say?'

No one answered me for a moment.

'It is nothing, Jennifer.' Philip was the first to speak. 'Here in Portugal there are many old superstitions about fires and the moon.' He turned to Theresa who was busily cleaning up the debris of shattered cups and spilled coffee. 'Leave that, Theresa. Bring more coffee. We will have it in the salon.'

'What has the moon to do with fire?' I asked.

'Nothing,' Neil said sharply. 'It is all nonsense.'

Philip shook his head. 'It is not nonsense. Everyone knows that some people are affected by the light from the moon. It makes people do very strange things.'

'Shut up,' Neil suddenly said. He shoved past his brother and went inside the castle.

'My brother is very sensitive to the phases of the moon,' Philip remarked after Neil had gone. 'If werewolves were in fashion today, Neil would make an excellent candidate.' He laughed to show that he was merely joking. 'Poor Neil,' he said. 'I am afraid I taunt him shamefully at times, but I feel it is for his own good. He is much too withdrawn, too sensitive. He must be shocked out of it sometimes.'

Carlotta was watching Philip with all the intensity of a mother hen worried over her chick. 'I don't think Jennifer is particularly interested in Neil's problems.' She got out of her chair. 'Shall we go in and have our coffee?'

'Yes, it's getting a bit chilly out here,' I said. For some reason or other I wanted to leave that terrace with its eerie torchlight. I wanted to run away from the moon and the shifting, restless water.

As I stood up, the handkerchief that Neil had given me fell from the sleeve of my dress. I wasn't aware it was gone until later.

Or perhaps I'd dropped it deliberately, if unconsciously. I didn't want it. In some odd way, it reminded me of death.

7

Neil was not in the salon where we had our coffee. In fact, he did not appear again for the remainder of the evening. He was not there to say goodnight when we left.

Philip drove us back to the villa. He asked if I would like to take a drive with him — the night was still young.

'Another time,' I told him. 'The trip to Lisbon was enough driving for me for one day. I'm a bit tired, really.' I wasn't making excuses. I would have liked to be alone with Philip, but I really was tired. The change in time was beginning to have its effect on me. I needed to rest.

'Of course, of course,' he whispered. He kissed my hand and Carlotta's. We left him and went indoors.

'What was all that gibberish about white fires on the moon?' Carlotta asked as we started toward our rooms.

'It was something Andy used to recite

to me. I don't know what on earth came over me, repeating it aloud the way I did. I didn't realize that I was doing it.'

'I'd watch my references in the future, if I were you, young lady. The Portuguese are a pretty superstitious lot, especially about the full moon. We Americans don't take superstitions seriously like they do here in Europe. It's almost a religion over here.' She was being quite serious.

'I'll be careful.'

I was no more than inside my room when Carlotta came back through the connecting door. 'Incidentally, give me another look at that handkerchief Neil claims belongs to you. I'm sure I've seen it someplace before.'

'Oh dear,' I said, showing an empty sleeve. 'I must have dropped it at the Alenquers'. Neil will think I'm playing Desdemona with him.'

'Are you?' Carlotta asked, narrowing her eyes suspiciously at me. 'It can prove a dangerous game. Remember what Othello did to his Desdemona.'

When she'd gone, I sighed and started to undress. I didn't want to think of anything but sleep. I slipped in between the crisp, fresh sheets. I could hear the ocean moving, rolling, lapping the shore. The moon streamed in through the windows and a gentle breeze billowed out of the lace curtains, making them flutter and dance in the room.

I had no trouble falling asleep, but my dreams were troubled ones. I saw Andrew's face looming over me, then the face smiled and it became Philip's face. I cradled my pillow and sighed contentedly. Suddenly the face changed again and a dark, cold mist swept over me. I shivered as I saw Neil staring at me through the fog. He was holding something in his hand. He held it out to me. It was a handkerchief, lacy and frilly. It was covered with blood.

I sat bolt upright in bed.

The moon was still large and bright. The house was as still as a tomb, nothing but silence all about me.

Suddenly I smelled smoke — but where was it coming from?

I leaped out of bed. Smoke was seeping in around the closed door to the hall. I snatched frantically for my robe and slippers and raced to the door. It may have been my vivid imagination, but the knob, even on the inside, felt warm as I touched it. I turned it and threw open the door.

Smoke billowed in upon me, forcing me back into the bedroom.

'Carlotta! Carlotta!' I yelled at the top of my lungs. 'Carlotta! My God, the house is on fire! Wake up!'

I must have been more rational than I gave myself credit for. I ran toward the bathroom and quickly soaked a bath towel until it was dripping wet. I slung it over my head, curling one end of the wet towel close to my nose and mouth. I knew that the towel would act as a kind of mask to protect my eyes and mouth from the deadly smoke.

'Carlotta!' I banged on the door. Oddly enough, it was locked — or so it seemed — from the inside.

As I dashed out into the hall, smoke enveloped me, cutting the air to nothing, choking my lungs, tearing my eyes to a burning madness.

'Carlotta, Carlotta!' I screamed, listening to the dreadful crackling sound that came from somewhere beneath us. I pounded frantically on the door to my aunt's room. The knob turned and I shoved it open. Carlotta's room was a mass of smoke and fumes. The fire, I decided, must have been in the lair directly under her bedroom. My eyes searched through the thick, swirling mass. Carlotta lay prone on the bed.

I dashed to her and shook her violently. Her eyes flickered open but I could see that she was already all but overcome by the smoke.

I grabbed a chair and threw it at the large French windows. The fragile panes of glass shattered and a welcome current of fresh air pulled at the smoke, but I knew the draft would soon draw the flames.

I rushed to the bed, wrapped Aunt Carlotta in the heavy soft comforter, and rolled her gently off the mattress, placing her on her back and forcing her mouth open. I began to provide mouth-to-mouth breathing. Carlotta stirred. I continued until her lungs were cleared enough for her to breathe again. It seemed like hours before I could help her into a sitting position and drag her to the shattered window, where she gulped in the cold night air greedily.

We couldn't stay where we were any longer. There was a tiny balcony off her bedroom, but no way to get down from it. Our only avenue of escape would be back through the house and downstairs.

I quickly soaked another towel for her and led her back through the smoke-filled bedroom and into the upstairs hall. The foyer was thick, too, with black smoke, but there were still no signs of flames, although the crackling sound was louder and more distinct once we started down the stairs.

We were almost to the front door, staggering and supporting one another, when the library doors were suddenly engulfed in flames.

I wrenched open the front door and shoved Carlotta out into the darkness. We stumbled across the lawn and collapsed a safe distance from the blazing villa. Carlotta lay on the wet grass, coughing violently. She tried to say something but the words wouldn't come.

We were both shivering in our night clothes.

The garage doors were open and Carlotta's car was in it. I dashed toward it but the car keys weren't in the ignition. They were most likely in the house somewhere. I snatched a beach blanket I found folded neatly on the back seat and ran back to where Carlotta lay. She looked weak, almost unconscious.

I took her in my arms and wrapped the blanket around us. We sat there shivering, saying nothing. We stared, transfixed, at the destruction being done before our very eyes. We were helpless. There was nothing we could do to save the villa from the ravages of the flames that ate away at it. Tears blinded me as I watched.

'Our home,' Carlotta groaned. 'Oh, Jen. Our home.' She collapsed against me in an agony of tears.

'Hush, Hush, Carlotta,' I found myself able to say, although my voice was shaking.

A man suddenly darted from around the back of the house and ran across the drive. I hadn't noticed it before — parked in a shadow along the drive was a long, dark limousine. It stood half-hidden beside the hedges.

'Carlotta!' I gasped. I pointed at the man running toward the limousine.

'Philip! Philip!' I yelled as loud as I could. The man stopped in his tracks and turned toward us. He stood quite still for a second or two, then started to run toward us. It wasn't Philip Alenquer, but his brother, Neil.

'Are you all right?' he asked, kneeling down beside us. 'I saw the flames and came as soon as I could,' he said.

I started to cry again; I couldn't help myself.

'The fire trucks should be here any moment. I called them before I left the castle,' he said.

'Fire trucks?' Carlotta stammered. 'You called the fire department?'

The question went unanswered. We heard the distant clanging of bells and sirens and within minutes the lawn was littered with men, vehicles and equipment. The idea of anyone making order out of such disorder was an absolute mystery to me. They worked fast and diligently, losing no time attacking their enemy, an enemy which would have destroyed a major part of Carlotta's life.

The trucks ruined the smooth, plush lawn. Ladders toppled a few statues and scraped the cypresses that lined the terrace. Then from out of nowhere came the echo of Carlotta's voice. I suddenly remembered something she'd uttered moments before. 'Our home,' she'd said. 'Our home.' I threw myself against her and burst into uncontrolled tears.

One of the men — I guessed him to be a fire official — started toward us. Neil rose and went to meet him. They spoke quietly at length.

'Of course they want to know how it started,' Neil began when he returned to Carlotta and me.

'We don't know,' I sobbed. 'We were both sound asleep.'

Carlotta clutched at me. 'Thank God you woke up, Jen. Thank God,' she cried and hugged me to her.

Neil looked uncomfortable. He shifted his weight from foot to foot 'Well,' he said, 'the firemen feel they got here in time. Of course they can't tell anything yet, but it appears that the fire is still contained on the lower floor. They don't believe it had a chance to reach the upper story. I certainly hope they are right.'

'It had just started up the main stairway when we got out,' I told him.

'That means nothing, really,' Neil remarked. 'The foyer is marble. It should contain the flames long enough for the firemen to do their work. Come, you must be freezing. Let's go sit in the limousine. I should have thought of it before. Forgive me. I am a fool.'

Numb with cold, terrorized by the horrible sight of the villa in flames, we struggled to our feet without a word and went toward the Alenquer limousine. Carlotta and I collapsed on the back seat as Neil produced a flask of brandy from the glove compartment. It helped warm us.

'Thank goodness you thought of the

fire department right away,' I said. Unconsciously I touched the back of Neil's hand. He pulled away.

'Yes, Neil,' Carlotta said in a weak tired voice, 'thank you.' Then as if it were an afterthought, she said something that made no sense to me. She said, 'Thank you, Neil — and I'm sorry.'

Whatever she meant, Neil understood. He nodded gravely and went to the trunk of the car to fetch a robe, which we tucked around us over the beach blanket.

As we watched the firemen at work, the warmth of the robe and blanket and the heat of the brandy rushing through my veins caused my reason to return bit by bit. I suddenly could not help but wonder how Neil could have seen the flames. The flames had not been visible even to Carlotta and me — and we had been inside the house.

Perhaps it was best not to ask any of the questions that suddenly occurred to me. Neil said he'd called the fire department before leaving the castle. Then he must have seen the flames from wherever he'd been in the castle. But that wasn't possible. From the Alenquer Castle Carlotta's villa was completely hidden from view, and the flames were confined to the inside of the villa.

And what was Neil doing running from the rear of the house? Why hadn't he tried to rescue us, if he was so concerned? Why was he running away when I spotted him?

I checked myself immediately. I was being too harsh. He more than likely had a very good explanation for everything.

I found Carlotta looking at me. I could tell that she was suddenly asking herself several of the same questions that were plaguing me. Unlike me, however, Carlotta spoke her mind.

'How could you have seen the fire from the castle?' she asked.

'I saw the smoke. I was up in one of the towers. I broke in through your back door when I got here and went up the service stairs, hoping to alert you both to the fire. I had seen the flames at the front of the villa and assumed the front of the house would be impossible to enter.'

I shook my head. 'I didn't know there were service stairs in the rear.'

'I found no one on the second floor.' Neil's voice faltered for a moment. 'I thought perhaps you both had gotten out and had gone for help.'

'But we were on the lawn when you ran to your car,' I said in a rush.

Neil avoided my eyes. 'Yes, I know. I saw you,' he admitted. 'I was — I was going to the car to get something to wrap you in,' he added.

'But — ' I started. Carlotta interrupted. 'Thank you, Neil. Thank you very much.'

I had many more questions but I felt Carlotta's interruption was intentional. She gave me a look that said 'I'll explain later' and began to cough again.

'Are you all right, Carlotta?' Neil asked. I explained the smoke inhalation.

'Perhaps we should drive over to the castle and get a doctor to look you over — both of you,' he said.

Carlotta held up a hand in protest. 'No, please. I want to stay here. I won't be able to rest until I know the extent of the damage.'

'There is no possible way to survey the

damage until morning,' he told her. 'The firemen will do a good job. Come. Let me take you both to the castle.'

'Oh, yes, you're right,' she said finally. 'Perhaps it is best that we get away from here. Actually, I don't think I can watch any more of this. It's too terrible.'

Neil slid behind the wheel and started the motor. He called out to one of the firemen, speaking to him in Portuguese. He most likely told him where he was taking us. They undoubtedly knew to whom the villa belonged and were well acquainted with Carlotta and the Alenquers.

It didn't seem possible that earlier this very night we had made the trip along this same road — happy, jovial. We were making the trip again, but now it was clouded with despair, anxiety, hopelessness.

'Tomorrow I will arrange for rooms at the inn in the village,' Neil said over his shoulder. Neither Carlotta nor I answered him. I frowned slightly. Why didn't he want us staying at the castle? It was certainly large enough.

The limousine stopped under the

portico. Philip was there to greet us. 'I heard the fire trucks. I saw the smoke,' he said. 'Are you all right?'

'Yes,' Carlotta assured him. 'But I'm afraid we can't say as much for my villa.'

'Oh, Carlotta. I am sorry,' Philip said softly. And he did look genuinely sorry, but in the next moment he shot Neil a fierce look. 'Have Theresa prepare supper for them in the salon. And have her fix up two guestrooms. Carlotta and Jennifer will be staying here.'

'I thought I would reserve rooms for them tomorrow at the inn,' Neil said.

'Nonsense. They'll stay here at the castle.'

The two men glared at one another briefly. Then Neil turned and went inside the castle. We heard him calling Theresa.

Morning was beginning to break as we straggled inside the old castle, settling ourselves before the fireplace in the salon. Theresa, looking sleepy and tired, hurried in with hot coffee. Philip laced it with more brandy as Carlotta and I, between us, told him what had happened.

Food was brought. It was a welcome

sight and we hastily attacked it with unbelievable appetites. We spoke very little while we ate.

Theresa came back some time later and told us that she had made up our rooms and to summon her when we wished to retire. I doubted very much whether I could sleep any more that night, but Philip insisted that I try.

I made certain Carlotta was bedded and comfortable before going to my room, directly across the hall from hers. I felt too keyed up to sleep, and went to the window, looking out over the ocean.

The moon had begun to descend toward the horizon. I knew it was only an illusion, but as I gazed at it, it really did look as if its surface was on fire.

8

I felt sure when I went to bed that I would not be able to sleep, but the next thing I knew it was daylight; the sun, bright and warm, shining through my window.

Someone had left a pink dressing gown and matching slippers. I thought as I slipped into the robe that it must have belonged to Neil's wife. It gave me an odd feeling to put it on.

I went across the hall to Carlotta's room. To my surprise, she was sitting up in bed eating from a tray.

'Well, you don't look the worse for wear,' I told her as I sat on the bed beside her. I kissed her cheek.

'Have a roll and some coffee,' she said. 'I'll ring for Theresa to bring another cup.' She eyed my ensemble. 'I see they dug up some old rags for you too.'

'I assume they once belonged to Neil's wife,' I told her.

'You're lucky. The only thing they found to fit me was something that belonged to Theresa. Now there's a gal with no style. How about some of my coffee?'

'No thanks. I'm not really hungry. I'll have some juice later on.' I studied her for a moment. 'You sure don't look like the same woman we put in that bed last night.'

'That was last night,' Carlotta said, waving a roll in front of my face before popping it into her mouth. 'The initial shock is over, finished, done. I can't sit around crying over spilled milk. There's a lot of work to be done.'

'You're a treasure,' I said. I could see why Carlotta was so successful in her career. She didn't accept defeat. A setback only made her forge ahead with more determination.

'Incidentally, I've had a telephone call already this morning,' Carlotta said. 'They surveyed the damage. It's not so bad.'

'Wonderful. What did they say exactly?'

'Several rooms downstairs are pretty well gutted. The lair is almost a complete loss. Of course there's a lot of smoke damage throughout, but the fire inspector told me it wasn't too bad. From the way he talked, the major part of the house is untouched. It can all be repaired, I suppose. I'll have to see it for myself before I decide what I'm going to do.'

'It sounds very encouraging,' I said.

Carlotta suddenly looked very serious. She leaned a bit forward and glanced around to make sure we couldn't be overheard. 'The rotten part is, that fire wasn't an accident,' she whispered.

'What do you mean?'

'They found evidence of foul play. He wants to see me at two o'clock. Don't ask me what it's all about; I'm just as bewildered as you are. Who the devil would want to burn down our villa? Is Philip or Neil around?'

'I haven't seen anyone.'

'We should go over to the villa and see what we can salvage. As long as the upstairs isn't badly damaged, at least we can cart out some clothes. Theresa brought me a few things and she said she hung some things in the closet in your room — probably nothing too stylish, but I don't think we have to worry about the way we look this morning.'

★   ★   ★

I found shoes and a dress hanging in the closet. They were certainly not to my taste — a bit loud and flashy — but I put them on and rejoined Carlotta. I had to laugh when I saw her in the somber black dress that was sizes too big for her. She laughed with me. Laughing, I found, helped lift my spirits.

'I wonder where everybody is?' she said when we'd come downstairs. 'Oh, Theresa, where are Neil and Philip?'

'Out, senhora. Both of them, I think.'

Carlotta frowned. 'I guess we'll just have to walk to the villa,' she said more to herself than to anyone

'But no,' Theresa put in. 'The small car, it is in the garage. Senhor Philip, he did not take his car.'

'Oh, good. I'm sure he won't mind our borrowing it for a little while. And we can have some girl talk on the way.'

* * *

In spite of Carlotta's remark about 'girl talk', the trip to the villa was made almost in silence. Carlotta drove slowly and carefully, her eyes glued to the twisting road.

I was thinking about the general layout of the land. 'Carlotta?' I said as we entered the gates of her villa. 'How could Neil have seen the smoke from his castle? That hill we just passed would hide your villa from view, wouldn't it?'

'I'm sure there's a perfectly good explanation, Jen. I wouldn't let it bother you.'

We fell silent again.

She parked the car at the top of the driveway, and we had our first daylight look at the scarred villa which had nearly become our funeral pyre. The face of the building was streaked with black soot. The windows were smashed in. Debris and remnants of the fire fighters' valiant efforts were strewn everywhere. However, in the brightness of day, the destruction did not appear as awful as it had during the night.

We climbed out of the car and stood gaping. The firemen must have tossed blazing pieces of furniture through the windows, by the looks of the debris that lay outside on the front terrace. The massive front door was burned and hanging on one hinge. We pushed our way through into the entrance hall.

Carlotta left me standing in the foyer and went off to inspect her lair. I didn't want to look. I knew it would be dreadful. I turned in the opposite direction and pushed hard on the now-warped doors of the drawing room. The interior of the room was practically untouched. Its articles of furniture sat peacefully on the thick, deep carpeting of the room. The smell of smoke was overwhelming, almost unbearable, but the room itself was virtually untouched by the hungry fire we had witnessed the night before.

I walked quickly through the living room and inspected the remaining rooms in that wing. They were all unblemished and in almost perfect condition, allowing for the smoke damage each room had suffered.

I retraced my steps, eager to share my

good news with Carlotta. She was standing in the doorway to the lair, staring straight ahead.

'Carlotta, come, look over here,' I called. 'Other than the lair and the entrance hall, everything seems fine.' I forcefully turned her away from the gutted lair, practically shoving her into the drawing room. The sight of the rooms worked like a charm. Her spirits were greatly improved as we finished inspecting that wing of the house.

'It's almost livable,' Carlotta said, breathing a sigh of relief. 'Let's go inspect the upstairs.' She tugged my arm.

We checked the rooms quickly, carefully, noting with relief and pleasure that except for the smoke damage the upstairs was mostly unscathed. As Carlotta rushed from room to room, opening and closing doors, she grinned happily. 'We could almost move back in,' she announced.

'Maybe that wouldn't be such a good idea,' I told her. 'I think we should wait until we hear what the fire inspection report says before jumping to any conclusions.'

'Yes, I guess you're right,' Carlotta

agreed reluctantly. 'But I sure hate being a house guest of the Alenquers. I guess I'm just the independent type.'

'I don't think Neil's too happy about our being there. Maybe we should just pack up and move to the inn,' I said.

'It might not be a bad idea.'

We started down the long stairway toward the front door. It seemed an eternity since last I descended these stairs hugging Carlotta close to me, trying to hold my breath, wrapping the damp towels around our heads.

'If the floors and ceilings are sound,' I told Carlotta, 'we can have the windows boarded up to cut out the drafts and close off the lair until we can get it repaired.'

She glanced at her watch. 'It's almost two o'clock. We should be heading for town. And while we're there, let's check on a suite at the inn. I don't think it was such a good idea of mine, tossing you at Philip the way I did.'

'You didn't really toss me at him. But if you want to know the truth, I don't mind at all.'

'That's what I'm afraid of. You aren't

taking him seriously, are you?'

'There's nothing to take him seriously about. I don't consider his trying to kiss me anything serious.'

'Well do me a favor. Don't get serious. It could be a mistake.'

★　★　★

We were late getting to the inspector's office. Several people were with him when we were ushered into his office. Two of the gentlemen present represented Carlotta's insurance company.

After dispensing with the opening formalities, Carlotta settled herself directly opposite the inspector. 'You said something about foul play this morning,' she said in English. 'What exactly did you mean?'

The inspector explained that they found that the fire had started in the study — the room Carlotta called her lair. 'In fact,' he pointed out, 'we can pinpoint the original blaze to the large table immediately under the front windows.'

'How can you possibly pinpoint the

start of a fire?' Carlotta asked.

The inspector propped his fingers under his chin. 'It is often impossible to find the actual cause of a fire unless gasoline or kerosene or defective wiring causes it. In this case, our inspection shows that gasoline had been poured on the table inside the windows. The can that contained the gasoline was found several hundred yards outside your property line, senhora, on the road to the west.'

'For a moment there,' Carlotta said, 'I was beginning to think you suspected me of burning down my own house — with me in it.'

'It has been done before, my dear lady. But you are both above suspicion. We have checked it all out. The gasoline can contained fingerprints. My men took the liberty of lifting sample fingerprints from the bedrooms you and your niece occupied. None of the prints match those on the gasoline container.'

'Who then?'

'That we do not know — yet.' He turned his attention to the male steno-grapher seated near him. The young man produced a document, copies of which he distributed to Carlotta and myself, handing the original to the inspector.

'This is a report of our findings,' the inspector explained. 'It will be necessary for us to go over the report in detail, and if you agree with everything we say concerning the damage, it will require your signature. Of course it makes no mention here of our findings relative to arson. You would have no way of substantiating that.'

It was nearly four thirty when we left the inspector's office and headed back toward Carlotta's villa. We had forgotten about stopping at the inn to rent rooms.

'We could go back,' I suggested.

'No, I'll drive in tomorrow after we've packed up our stuff from the villa and I have my own car,' Carlotta said. 'I'm sure another night at the castle won't do us any harm.'

Later, I was to remember her remark, and realize how wrong it had been.

9

I slept badly that night.

Neil had disappeared somewhere. Philip seemed concerned but not overly so. Carlotta was uncomfortable and anxious to move to the village inn.

I kept thinking of the fire inspector's report. A gasoline can, found on the road leading west. That would be on the road leading to Alenquer Castle.

I gave up on my attempts to fall asleep and got up instead, slipping into my robe. A warm spring breeze fluttered the curtains and I went out onto the balcony.

It was a lovely night. The moon was full. Again I thought its pewter surface looked as if it were bathed in white fire.

I wasn't the only one admiring the full moon. When I looked down I saw a man below, his head turned upward. The scar on his cheek seemed to glow under the light.

What on earth was Neil doing? As I

watched, he moved, leaning forward and picking up several small stones. He threw them, one by one, at a tree a short distance away. With each new throw he used greater and greater force until the stones were smashing hard into the bark, splintering it as they hit. With all the wildness of a man possessed, he flung the last stone. It shattered against the tree and I heard Neil groan as though completely enraged.

'Neil,' I called, concerned. He was obviously extremely distressed and agitated.

He whirled around and looked up at me. We stood looking at each other for a fraction of a second.

'Is anything the matter?' I called down softly.

He didn't answer, but turned and ran as fast as he could into the trees.

'Wait!' I ran back into my room, down the hall, down the stairs and out into the garden. 'Neil?' He was nowhere in sight. 'Neil!'

I heard a twig snap behind me and turned.

'Jennifer.' Philip came toward me, his expression one of concern. 'What on earth are you doing roaming around out here? Did I hear you call Neil?'

'Yes. He seemed upset about something. I thought talking with someone might help calm him, but he ran away.'

Philip only smiled. 'My brother is a strange man, Jennifer. He does and says strange things. You must not pay any attention to him.' He fumbled in his pocket for cigarettes, and lit one. 'I'm glad you couldn't sleep,' he said. 'We have not had much of a chance to be alone these past few days, what with Carlotta and Neil being about.'

'Carlotta is under a terrible strain. I want to be with her as much as possible. She needs all the help she can get right now.'

'You don't know your aunt very well. She is a very independent individual.'

'But even independent people need companionship when things aren't going well.'

'Yes, I suppose you are right. Still, I've been a little envious of your constant attention to her. You have been avoiding me, I feel.'

I smiled at him as warmly as I could. 'Now why should I do that — avoid you?'

'Perhaps it is because you like me too much.'

I laughed. 'Are all European men so conceited?'

'I am not conceited.' He flicked his cigarette away. 'It is only that I feel you like me a little. I hope I am right.' Suddenly he turned me toward him, his hands tight on my arms. 'Do you like me, Jennifer — a little?'

My smile faded. He looked more handsome than ever before. His lids were lowered, his lips slightly parted. My heart beating faster, my pulse raced.

'Yes,' I said softly. 'I like you — I like you very much.'

He pulled me into his arms. 'Oh, Jennifer,' he whispered as he hugged me close. He didn't try to kiss me. He merely held me tight. I found myself clinging to him. The strain I had been under was beginning to take hold of me. I could feel his breath against my hair, the touch of his cheek against mine.

'Jennifer,' he whispered again. He was

going to kiss me and I wanted him to. I wanted everything to be all right again. I dreaded the nightmares, the loneliness I'd faced after Andy left me. I wanted to be loved, needed, wanted.

The night grew quiet as our lips touched. The kiss was soft and lingering. 'Philip,' I murmured.

Suddenly I had an image of myself in the arms of a man I hardly knew — because I was lonely, because I was on the rebound, because of an endless stream of bad reasons. I tore myself from Philip's arms.

'Jennifer — what is it?' Again he tried to pull me back into his arms.

'No, please, Philip. This isn't right.'

'What is not right, my darling?' He tried to kiss me again but I turned my head. 'I love you, Jennifer.'

'But you can't. You hardly know me.'

'I know you well enough to love you. Come, let us stroll in the garden. It is so lovely — like you. I promise I will be good,' he said with a charming, boyish smile.

I let him lead me down the wide stone steps, out into the beautiful moonlit garden. The truth was, I didn't want to be alone. I wanted to be with someone, talk to someone. I wanted to forget the past.

But I was only half-dressed, alone in the dark with a man I barely knew. I stopped and reached for his hand. 'I must go in, Philip. I shouldn't be out here with you. It isn't proper.'

'We are doing nothing to be ashamed of,' he said. His eyes held mine. 'I love you, Jennifer. I think I fell in love with you the first time I saw you.'

'Oh, Philip, you mustn't. It can't be.'

'Why can it not be? You are a beautiful woman. I am a man who loves you very much. What is so wrong with that? Are you still thinking about the man in America?'

'Yes. No, that isn't it. It's just that everything is happening much too fast. When I fall in love I want my eyes to be wide open. I don't want to get hurt again, Philip. Can you understand that?'

'I would never hurt you, my darling.' Again he pulled me into his arms.

I looked up at him. He was everything I'd ever wanted in a man: tall, strong, virile, handsome, polite. He was delightful company, fun to be with. Conversation came easily. He was intelligent and, I gathered from past conversation, industrious. And he said he loved me.

Yet deep inside there was something that told me to take care. It was Andrew Fuller's voice warning me. I could see Andy's face mouthing promises. Now I could see the deceit behind his eyes, deceit I hadn't seen when I should have been looking for it. Andrew Fuller had left an indelible scar and I knew it would be a while before that scar would heal and disappear, if it ever would disappear. I looked into Philip's eyes and saw no deceit — but then I hadn't seen it in Andrew's either.

'Stop thinking about him,' Philip said. 'It is not good to live in the past. You made a mistake once. Do not carry it with you forever. It can only hurt you, Jennifer. I will make you forget your American.'

A cloud suddenly passed over the moon, darkening the garden for a moment. Philip stared up at it, an odd expression on his face.

'Come,' he said. 'You must go in. You will catch cold.'

As we turned back toward the castle the cloud drifted from the face of the moon, illuminating the garden. A sudden movement caught my eye. I glanced toward the trees. Standing there, staring at us, was Neil. How long he'd been watching us I didn't know, but from the look on his face, he'd been there a good while watching, listening.

When he saw me glance at him he stepped back into the shadow of the trees. Philip hadn't seen him, but Philip had felt me stiffen.

'What is it?' he asked.

I shook my head. 'Nothing,' I said. 'Nothing at all.'

But it was something — something that troubled me because I could not understand it.

10

If sleep had been difficult earlier, it was virtually impossible now. Things seemed to have become increasingly complicated. I couldn't afford to fall in love with Philip Alenquer. Yet, I felt that I was falling in love with him. Carlotta would label it a rebound love — and she would probably be right. Everything was jumbled up inside my head. Also, Carlotta had warned me against falling in love with Philip. Why?

And why had Neil been spying on us?

Despite Carlotta's old friendship with the Alenquers, I felt she did not want me getting involved with them. Marrying Philip would involve me totally.

'Marry?' I said, blinking open my eyes. *My, you are rushing things*, I told myself. *You only met him a few days ago.* Philip had said he loved me; he hadn't said he wanted to marry me.

I was drifting off finally. Then suddenly

my eyes flew open again. I heard something. It sounded like someone breathing heavily somewhere in my room. I sat up in the bed and looked around. There was an orange-red glow at the windows.

'Oh, no,' I cried. 'Not again.'

I jumped out of bed and rushed to the windows. Outside in the center of the garden a log rested atop one of the small stone benches. It was blazing brightly. Someone had obviously soaked it in kerosene or gasoline and had ignited it. The flames were harmless enough; the bench was well isolated from the trees and woods. But from where I stood looking down, it reminded me of an altar sacrifice. It was eerie and horrible, making me shiver with fear.

I had almost forgotten the sound that had brought me out of my sleep. Then I heard it again at my back. I turned from the blazing fire and tried to peer into the blackness of the room. 'Who's there?' I called nervously.

There was no answer, but the breathing continued. It sounded closer.

I snatched up my robe and started toward the light switch. A hand suddenly went around my mouth. I could feel a man's strength forcing me toward the bed. I clutched and clawed but he was too much for me. He pitched me onto the bed. I lay there, horror-stricken. I couldn't see anything but the outline of a man's body standing over me.

'Be careful, Angelica,' his voice said. It was a rasping, terrifying voice; one I'd never heard before. 'You will not get away from me again,' he said. Then he laughed low in his throat and backed slowly away. I lay unmoving on the bed, petrified with fear. I saw the door open and the man's outline back through it. The door closed and he was gone.

I stared. I could do nothing. I was paralyzed with fright.

Then the fire outside blazed more brightly, and before I knew what I was doing I started to scream.

Suddenly Carlotta was bending over me. I scarcely remember Theresa hurrying through the doorway, tying the rope of her dressing robe around her. Then

Philip's face materialized, as if by magic.

'She's hysterical,' I heard Carlotta say. Carlotta's hand flashed out and slapped me soundly across the face. I collapsed into a heap of tears. Carlotta gathered me into her arms. 'There, there, child. You've been dreaming. It's only a nightmare. Calm yourself. Calm yourself, dear.'

I clung to her, sobbing away my hysteria. 'A man,' I sobbed. 'A man in my room. The fire. Fire.' My eyes were wide with terror.

'It's all right, Jen. The villa's all right — there's no fire anymore. You were having a nightmare, that's all. It's all right.'

'No, no,' I sobbed. 'There was a man, here, in my room. He spoke to me. He threatened me.'

Carlotta's back went straight. 'A man? Here in your room?'

'It wasn't a dream, Carlotta. I saw him. I saw a man standing over me. He threw me across the bed. He threatened me.'

'Who? Who was standing over you? Who threatened you?'

I shook my head violently. 'I don't

know. A man. Just a man; I didn't see his face.'

'But surely you knew his voice, his shape. What man, Jen?'

'I don't know. I don't know,' I wailed, again collapsing against her.

I didn't see Carlotta look up to Philip or he down to her. I didn't see Theresa staring at me, then slowing moving her eyes to Carlotta and Philip, questioning.

Neil suddenly dashed through the door. 'What is going on here?' he demanded.

'Jennifer had a nightmare,' Carlotta said, trying to pass over what I'd said. 'It's all right. Go back to bed.'

'No, No,' I insisted. 'It wasn't a nightmare. I saw him. He was standing over me.'

'Who?' Neil demanded.

I looked up at him. My eyes widened. The frame, the shape, it all looked familiar. I couldn't speak. I cringed away from him.

'She doesn't know,' Carlotta said to Neil. 'She claims there was a man in her room threatening her.'

Philip seated himself beside me and

pulled me from Carlotta's arms into his. His lips brushed my hair. 'Go back to sleep, Jen. Would you like Theresa to bring you something to help you sleep?'

'You don't believe me, any of you,' I sobbed.

'Of course I believe you. It is just that . . . ' He left his sentence unfinished.

'The fire,' I said, my eyes suddenly darting toward the windows. 'Out there on the lawn. An altar fire.'

'A what?' Carlotta gasped.

Neil moved toward the window. Carlotta and Theresa followed. 'There is nothing out there,' Carlotta said. 'What on earth are you talking about now?' She sounded annoyed with me.

I shoved Philip away and ran to the window. The bench below was white and naked. There was no sign of a blazing log, no sign of flames or smoke. Everything was as it had been. There was no fire.

'I saw it.' I looked beseechingly toward Neil. His eyes bored into mine. I backed away. 'There was a fire burning in the garden.'

'Jennifer,' Carlotta said sharply, 'you're

working yourself into a state of hysteria. You were merely having a bad dream. I'll get you a pill. Get back in bed and forget this nonsense. You just had a nightmare.'

I knew she was being sharp for my own good, but my distress increased. I looked toward Philip. 'But it wasn't a nightmare, Philip. It wasn't. I saw the fire. I saw the man in my room. I heard him threaten me.'

'What did he say?' Philip asked, trying to sound patient and understanding.

'He called me Angelica.'

Carlotta, who was halfway out of the room, stopped dead in her tracks. She whirled around and stared at me. She started to say something. Then I saw her stiffen her back again, turn and go across the hall to her own room. No one spoke. Everyone seemed to be staring at me as though I'd just uttered the most awful profanity.

Suddenly I remembered — Angelica was the name of Neil's dead wife. 'Angelica,' I breathed, looking straight into Neil's eyes. He stared back for a moment, then turned and strode out of the room.

Carlotta hurried back into the room with a glass of water and a sleeping tablet. 'Here, take this,' she said brusquely. She held out the pill. I wanted to disobey her but the look on her face brooked no denial.

Meekly, I took the pill and swallowed it with water. Carlotta eased me back onto the pillows and covered me up. She motioned to Theresa and Philip, who withdrew without a word.

'Now you get some sleep, Jen,' she said. 'The pill should knock you out for a good while. I'll stay with you until you fall asleep.'

I could feel my eyelids getting heavy already.

'Do you want me to stay here with you all night?' Carlotta asked. 'That bed's big enough for four.'

'I'd like that,' I said sleepily.

I heard the door close as Philip and Theresa left us. I felt Carlotta slip in between the sheets.

And that was the last I heard or felt. Morpheus took me into his arms and carried me off.

11

I awoke to the merry chirping of birds outside my window. The world seemed completely changed. Everything sparkled like a shiny new penny. Even my thoughts seemed lighter, more cheerful. I purposely refused to dwell on what had happened the night before.

Theresa was in the kitchen, humming to herself. When I entered she turned from the sink where she was peeling potatoes. She smiled at me.

'Ah, senhorita. And how are you feeling this beautiful day?'

I smiled back. 'Fine, thank you, Theresa.'

'Good, good. Come, I have some breakfast saved for you. You are hungry, no?'

'I am hungry, yes.'

We laughed together. I was determined to be cheerful. Theresa, I felt, was who I needed this morning — a simple, uncomplicated woman. She set a place for me at the kitchen table. As she busied herself with getting the food set before me, she said, 'Your aunt, she tells me she is going to see someone in the village. She tells me she will not be back for many hours.'

'And where are the menfolk?'

'Ah, that I do not know, senhorita. Senhor Philip I think is also in the village on business, or perhaps he is at one of the tenant farms. Senhor Neil . . . ' She shrugged her shoulders. 'Who knows? He comes, he goes. I am never sure he is living here at all.'

'Yes, I know what you mean. He is rather the tall, dark, silent type, isn't he?'

Theresa frowned at me as she translated my English. 'Ah, yes. I see. Tall, dark and silent. That describes him very well, senhorita.' She kept repeating the phrase as she went back to her work. 'Tall, dark and silent.'

'It certainly is a lovely afternoon,' I commented, looking out at the clear blue sky and the bright, warm sunshine. A soft breeze was tickling the tops of the fir trees. 'I think I'll go for a swim later on.

The water looks so clear and inviting.'

'Oh no, senhorita. No swim here. Very bad here. The current sometimes brings the sharks very close. It is very dangerous. You must no swim here.'

My brow crinkled slightly. 'But Aunt Carlotta says — '

'Your aunt lives around the bend of the beach. For some reason sharks do not go there; the water is warmer or something. They must like it colder, like here.' She swept potato peelings into a piece of newspaper, wadded it up and dropped it into a trash basket. 'You have sharks in America?'

'Oh yes. Fortunately where I come from, they only live in aquariums.'

Whether she understood what I said or not, I don't know. She nodded and continued with her work.

We chatted about America while I finished my breakfast. Afterward I relaxed over coffee, listening to Theresa talk about her family, her years of service to the Alenquers.

'Then you knew Angelica?' I asked.

She froze for a second, staring out of the window over the sink. 'Yes,' she said after a long time. 'I knew her. Too bad. A

148

beautiful girl, but very fiery.'

'Were she and Neil married long?' I wasn't really trying to gossip with Theresa; I was only making conversation. Theresa unfortunately decided I was prying.

'Please excuse me, senhorita, but I am afraid I must attend to the bedrooms now. The day is getting late.'

I flushed slightly and put my coffee cup down on the saucer. 'Yes, of course,' I said. I felt embarrassed at having my questions misunderstood.

'You take a nice walk in the gardens. They are very lovely. You will enjoy. The view is good.'

'Yes, perhaps I will,' I said as I got up and started out of the kitchen.

'Senhorita,' Theresa said as I started away. I turned.

'The Senhora Angelica. It would not be wise to speak her name here. There is much Senhor Neil wishes to forget — Senhor Philip too.'

I smiled kindly. 'Thank you, Theresa. I understand. I am sorry I brought it up. Forgive me.'

She shrugged her shoulders again and

grinned. 'You are a very nice lady. I am glad you have come to visit us.'

As I started out into the afternoon sun, I couldn't help but feel the terrible memories of last night sweeping back toward me. I tried to fend them off but they pushed away the mist with which I'd tried to cover them. Angelica's name kept bouncing back and forth inside my head. Everyone seemed so hesitant to speak of her. I was convinced that the mystery surrounding her death was indeed evil. Of course, Theresa was merely being a loyal employee and I had had no right to try to pry information out of her. I hadn't meant to, but innocent as I had been, I felt guilty about it.

I suddenly heard the rasping, whispering voice speak Angelica's name. I knew I was imagining it, but it seemed as real now as it had the night before. I hadn't been dreaming last night. I'd seen a man looming over me. I'd seen the fire blazing on the garden bench.

A sudden realization struck me. The fire. The garden bench. I started determinedly toward the back garden, the garden that lay beneath my bedroom window. I had to find out. I had to satisfy my own doubts. It hadn't been a bad dream. It had happened and I was suddenly intent upon proving it, if not to the others at least to myself.

The bench was exactly where I had remembered it. There was no sign of burnt wood on it now, but as I got closer I noticed that it looked unusually clean compared with the other stone benches that dotted the garden. I ran my hand over the surface. My hand came away perfectly clean. I frowned slightly. A bench sitting out in the weather, such as this one, would at least have a bit of grit on it. But this bench was clean, as though it had recently been washed and scrubbed.

I sat down on it, leaning my elbows on my knees. Then my eye settled on a small chunk of charred wood resting alongside one of the side supports. I bent forward and picked it up. It was a small bit, but there wasn't the slightest doubt that it was charred wood. And it was soggy wet.

I tightened my hand around it, oblivious to the smudges it made on my palm. There wasn't the slightest doubt in my mind now. I had seen a fire. I hadn't imagined the blaze. And if the fire were real then the man in my room was real, too, and he had loomed over me and threatened that I wouldn't get away from him again. I knew I hadn't dreamed it, but the suspicions of the others had managed to make me doubt myself for a while — but not now.

I pushed the piece of charred wood into the pocket of my skirt, with the intention of showing it to Carlotta when she returned from the village.

Carlotta. Why had she gone to the village? What business was she on?

The inn, of course, I told myself. She wanted to be away from Alenquer Castle and had most likely gone to reserve rooms for us. But why hadn't she simply telephoned the inn? Perhaps she had gone to see the insurance people. Or perhaps she had to go to make a deposit on our rooms.

My episode with Philip in the garden last night came back to me and suddenly I didn't really want to leave Alenquer

Castle all that soon. But I wouldn't be far away, I told myself. It wasn't as though I were returning to America.

I left the garden, walking blindly, just as I had walked away the night Andrew Fuller broke our engagement. I was trying to escape thoughts of Andy and Philip and the decision I would eventually be forced to make.

I turned left around the corner of the side terrace and went toward the sea. I saw a footpath and took it without knowing where it led. I found myself in a deep grove, thick with heavy-barked trees and tangled undergrowth. The path was narrow and hard to navigate, but I pushed my way on, hoping I'd eventually reach the cliff where I could look out over the clear, blue ocean and let the wind blow away my unhappy thoughts.

I walked for a short distance. Through the trees I saw a clearing ahead. The sun was shining down on what looked like a cottage. I lifted a low-hanging branch and peered at the structure. It was indeed a cottage. It must have been charming at one time, but now, unfortunately, the roof was gone and the windows were smashed, the walls streaked black.

I stepped into the clearing. The door was gone from its hinges. I looked inside. The interior was nothing but a burned-out shell. Ashes, dirt and soot were everywhere. Charred remains of furniture were barely recognizable. A stairway that had gone up to a second level was gutted and falling to ashes.

'What are you doing here?'

Startled, I whirled around and found Neil glaring at me. He looked like someone possessed. His fists were clenched. The ugly scar on the left side of his face seemed to pulse and throb as his eyes bored into me.

'What are you doing, I said?' he demanded, grabbing me by the wrist. His hand felt as though he were capable of crushing the bone with very little effort.

I wrenched free, or tried to.

'Get back to the house. Get out of here, do you hear?' He shoved me away from him.

I rushed headlong into the grove of trees, not seeing, not caring where I was going. I just wanted to get away from him. I ran blindly, not looking, not seeing where I was going.

My foot suddenly slipped into a hole. The toe of my other foot connected with a sharp rock and I pitched forward, flat on my face. I screamed. I couldn't move for a moment.

I felt Neil's hand on my shoulder. I turned and looked up at him, terrified. He reached for me. I struggled, but I was no match for him. He lifted me as easily as he had lifted my heavy luggage at the airport. He carried me out through the grove, back toward the castle.

'I am sorry,' he said softly as he carried me in his arms. 'I should not have frightened you as I did. It is just that . . . ' He did not finish. He walked like a man with a duty to perform that he wanted to get done and have finished.

He carried me through the garden and up onto the terrace. Gently, as though I were the most fragile thing in all the world, he laid me down on a chaise.

'Theresa!' he bellowed back over his shoulder as he knelt to examine my ankle.

No one answered. He called again, yelling something in Portuguese, all the while testing the tenderness of my bruise. 'It does not seem to be broken,' he said. 'It is merely sprained. I will get something to tape it.'

The minute he was out of sight I tried to get up. I wanted to run away as far as I possibly could. I wanted to hide until Carlotta returned, until Philip returned. When I stood, the pain in my ankle was excruciating. I sank back onto the chaise and tried not to cry. It wasn't the pain that was bringing the tears; it was my fear. When I saw Theresa hurrying along beside Neil, however, I felt a little more relieved. Together they examined my ankle, exchanging a constant flow of Portuguese, and Neil proceeded to wrap it in a bandage while Theresa went back inside.

'I have told Theresa to call the doctor and have him come at once.'

'No, please. I'm all right. I don't think I need a doctor,' I managed to say.

'Lay back, Jennifer. Relax. I will not harm you.'

A tiny pressure gripped my throat. He had called me Jennifer. He had said my name. Suddenly I could feel my fear draining away. I began to relax.

As he wrapped the bandages securely around the injured ankle, I studied his hair, his face, his hands. He wasn't as young or as smoothly handsome as Philip, yet there was something about him that was more attractive. He had his head lowered so the scar on his face was obscured. His hair curled in an unruly mop all over his head. His complexion was bronzed from many hours in the sun. I found myself watching the point of hair that hung down over the collar of his shirt. Neil moved his head back and forth as his fingers wound the bandages round and round my ankle.

'There,' he said, fastening the bandage securely. 'I think that will have to do until the doctor gets here. Now I would suggest you stay where you are and try to relax.' He turned and started away.

'Neil,' I said quickly, suddenly not wanting him to go.

He turned, his eyes soft now. 'Yes?'

For want of something to say, I simply said, 'Thank you. I'm sorry if I've been a bother.'

'You are not a bother, Jennifer,' he said. He smiled and his whole face changed. But the smile vanished almost as quickly as it had come. His eyes widened as he looked at me. He was staring at something on my face. He came toward me so quickly that I found myself cringing again.

'Hold still,' he warned. He put his hands alongside my head, turning my face toward the sun. He brushed back my hair. 'You have cut yourself,' he said with concern. He pulled a handkerchief from his back pocket and began to clean away the trickle of blood running down my temple. 'I will get something to clean it.'

Again he was gone. This time I did not try to stand up and run away. I wanted to talk to him, befriend him, show him that I understood.

'This may sting a little,' he said as he dabbed something onto my cut. It did. I cringed and tried not to cry out. 'You are a very brave girl,' he said with a faint smile on his lips. 'I usually bellow like an injured calf when Theresa subjects me to this medicine.'

I laughed softly. 'That seems hard to believe — you complaining of pain.' I hoped he wouldn't misconstrue my remark.

'I do not like pain. I prefer bellowing. It relieves the frustrations.'

I knew what he meant. There had been so many, many times of late when I wanted to stand with clenched fists and scream. I had almost forgotten those times, but now Neil had brought them to my mind again. Suddenly I knew how he must have felt — still felt.

'This is the third time you've come to my rescue. Do you realize that?'

'The third time?' he said as he continued to treat the cut.

'The airport, the beach, and now here.'

'The beach?' he said. He spoke the word gravely but there was a certain pleasant lightness in his tone.

'The day you shot at me. Theresa told me about the sharks. You were merely trying to warn me off, weren't you?'

His hand stopped, poised over the cut.

His face was serious. 'I called to you but you didn't hear me. I am a very good marksman, so I decided the bullet was the quickest way to convey my message and discourage you from swimming in our waters.'

I laughed in spite of myself. 'You conveyed your message all right. You nearly scared the wits out of me.'

'That was what I intended to do, senhorita.'

I looked into his face. It was very close to mine and his hands felt like polished velvet against my skin. 'I would prefer it if you continued to call me Jennifer. It sounds so much nicer than senhorita.'

I saw his lips twitch as though tempted to smile. 'Are you always so good at getting men to do what you say?'

'Not always,' I answered, trying to sound flippant. *Good heavens, Jennifer*, I admonished myself, *you're flirting with him — you're flirting with him.*

Philip came out onto the terrace just then. 'What are you doing, Neil?' he demanded.

Neil didn't answer. He turned back

toward me and examined the cleaned cut on my temple. Philip came swiftly toward us and snatched the handkerchief out of Neil's hand. 'Leave that alone,' he said sharply. 'You are no doctor.' Neil glared at him for a moment, then moved away.

Philip sat down beside me and took my hand. His face was kind. 'Theresa told me you had a slight accident and that the doctor is on his way. Are you all right, my darling?'

'Yes, it was nothing. I tripped in the grove.'

'You poor darling.' He tried to pull me into his arms but something inside me resisted him. I felt embarrassed with Neil there watching. When I looked at Neil I saw he was scowling. He turned away and walked quickly back into the castle.

'How did this happen?' he asked, touching first the cut on my temple then glancing down to my sprained ankle.

'I was walking in the grove. I tripped. Neil carried me here and told Theresa to call a doctor. I didn't want him to but he insisted.'

'I agree with Neil,' Philip said. 'You

161

must have a doctor examine you.'

'But it's merely a sprain. I'm fine, really I am.'

'You lay back and relax until the doctor arrives.' He eased me back on the chaise. He sat there studying me for a moment, smiling, but the smile faded. 'Why were you walking with Neil in the grove?'

'I wasn't. I fell and I must have screamed when I twisted my ankle. He heard me and carried me here.'

'What were you and Neil talking about just now?' He tried to make his question sound casual, but I could see by the look in his eyes that it was very important to him.

'Nothing much, really. Just that — ' I cut myself off. I didn't think I should talk about Neil's shooting at me, even though I knew now it was only a means of protecting me. I didn't want to aggravate Philip. That there was some ill feeling between him and his brother was evident. 'We just talked, that's all.'

Philip gave me a suspicious look. 'I do not want you associating with Neil, Jennifer. He is not altogether right

162

sometimes. He has been known to have terrible fits of temper. He might do you harm without realizing it. He is not accountable for certain of his actions.'

'He seemed perfectly all right just now.'

'Yes, he is perfectly all right at times, but then the least little thing might turn him into a raving madman. It has all to do with the unfortunate business with Angelica, his wife.' Philip shook his head. 'Be careful when around Neil, please, darling. Do it as a favor to me.'

'But I really don't think Neil could harm anyone.'

'Please,' Philip insisted. 'Stay away from him. He can be very deceiving and very dangerous.'

I didn't have an opportunity to promise or to withhold my promise. Theresa came scurrying out with a dark-bearded doctor close at her heels.

12

I was propped up in bed writing my long overdue letters home when Carlotta came in. 'Philip told me what happened,' she said, hurrying over to me. 'I have to call and cancel the rooms at the inn. They say you're supposed to stay in bed for a couple of days.'

'Nonsense,' I told her. 'I'm fine. It's only a minor sprain. It's nothing at all.'

'Doctor's orders,' she said, leveling a finger at me. 'You stay in bed.' She fussed with my pillows and flecked imaginary dust from the night table.

I watched her for a moment. 'Carlotta?' I said, pausing to phrase my question carefully so that she'd think it was merely casual. 'What is that burned-out cottage?'

She turned sharply, a trace of a frown on her brow. 'What burned-out cottage?'

'The one in the grove. I came across it today when I was out walking.'

'Oh, that cottage,' she said, returning to

her straightening. 'Neil used to use it as a studio. It burned down.'

'A studio? What kind of studio?'

'He's a botanist. He used to teach at the University of Coimbra.'

'Neil, a botanist? That's hard to believe. He certainly doesn't seem the type of man to be interested in trees and plants and things like that.'

Carlotta merely shrugged indifferently.

'How did the cottage catch fire?' I persisted.

'No one knows. They think Angelica fell asleep with a cigarette in her hand.' She kept her back to me.

I bit my lower lip. Something was suddenly clear. Angelica obviously died in that cottage. That was why Neil was so upset about my being there. Now I understood. I had to smile to myself in spite of the gruesomeness surrounding the cottage — Neil seemed intent upon scaring me off every time we encountered one another.

'Angelica's death was accidental then?'

Carlotta did not look at me. 'That was the verdict. Death by accident.'

'Yet there are some who suspect Neil of killing her?'

Carlotta said nothing. She was holding one of my hair brushes in her hand. Suddenly she dropped it on the dressing table. 'Enough of that,' she said flatly, turning to face me. 'Such conversation had best be left alone. And I suggest you stay clear of Neil Alenquer. He's . . .' Her eyes moved toward the door. Neil was standing in the open doorway. His face was ashen. He was looking at Carlotta with smoldering disapproval.

Carlotta gathered her pride together. 'I'm sorry, Neil,' she said boldly. Then she sidled past him and left the room. Her face was the color of blood.

Neil simply stood there with his hands behind his back. He didn't move but he turned his eyes on me and his expression softened. If he were angry it was with Carlotta and not with me.

'Is your ankle bothering you?' he asked.

I shook my head. 'It's fine. The doctor said I had just turned it. It's only a slight sprain.'

'Good.' He stood looking at me for a

long time. 'I brought you this,' he said, producing my beach robe from behind his back. He laid it at the foot of the bed and started out of the room.

'Neil,' I called softly. He turned back. 'Don't be annoyed with Carlotta. She meant no harm. She was explaining about the cottage.' His steady gaze made me flounder. 'I didn't know,' I said for want of something better to say.

He came back to the bed and stood beside me. 'Of course,' he said. His voice was kind and gentle. He reached out and took my hand and raised it to his lips. My whole being started to tremble.

'How gallant,' Philip said sarcastically from the doorway. 'But I would appreciate it very much if you would refrain from your hand-kissing until after the wedding.'

I shot Philip a surprised look.

Neil dropped my hand and stared at me for a moment. I could feel the color rising in my face, right up to my hairline. Neil turned on his heels and stomped out. But he looked more frightened than angry.

'Oh, Philip,' I sighed. 'You shouldn't have said that. I never — '

'I know, I know,' he said, seating himself on the side of the bed. He took my hand. 'I was being impulsive.' He touched my hand to his cheek. 'I just wanted Neil to know the situation between you and me.'

'But there is no 'situation', as you put it. You've never proposed and I have never accepted.'

'Then I propose now, Jennifer. Please. Marry me. I love you very, very much.'

'Oh, Philip,' I said, squeezing his hand. 'Please don't ask me. Not yet, anyway. I'm not sure. I don't want to rush into anything.'

'You prefer Neil perhaps,' he said, suddenly annoyed.

'Good heavens, I don't mean that I prefer Neil. It's just that I'm still trying to get over Andrew. There's nothing between Neil and me — nothing. How could there be? We hardly know each other, hardly speak to each other.'

'Perhaps you do not think so, but I know my brother. He has always tried to take everything away from me. It has been like that since we were children. Whatever was Neil's was Neil's; whatever was mine was Neil's also.' Philip wasn't looking at me. 'And now that he knows I am in love with you, he wants you for himself. Well, he will not take you away from me, Jennifer. I will not let him take you away.' He wrenched his hand from mine and rushed out of the bedroom.

I called to him. I started to go after him. but the moment I stepped onto the floor I was reminded of the pain in my ankle. I called to him again, but he didn't come back.

I lay back against the pillows and shielded my eyes with my forearm. Would things ever clear up for me? I wondered. Every hour, every day brought more complications.

I glanced at my unfinished letter and suddenly longed to be away from it all. Yet, I reminded myself, going home wouldn't solve anything for me. The memories there were just as bitter. At least here in Portugal I didn't have to face those well-meaning friends who, when they looked at me, looked at me as a woman who'd been jilted. I couldn't face that — my pride wouldn't let me.

The room was suddenly stifling. Carefully I got out of bed and hopped toward a chair near the French doors leading to the balcony. I seated myself, feeling a small lump in the pocket of my skirt. I slipped my hand inside the pocket and took out the piece of charred wood. I looked at it for a long time and then, without really knowing why, the cinder repulsed me. I threw it out over the balcony, down into the garden where I'd found it.

What's the use? I said to myself. What difference did it make? Nothing made sense anyway. At least I knew there'd been a blazing log on top of that bench, and that was all that was important. I didn't have to prove anything to the others.

My eyes wandered to the terry cloth beach robe draped across the bottom of the bed. I suddenly wondered about the handkerchief I'd kicked under the chair on the terrace. Had Neil found it? It must have been one of hers — one of Angelica's. Neil was obviously aware, and had been for a long time, of how Carlotta felt toward him. But why did Carlotta feel the way she did? What was there about Angelica's death that made her suspect Neil of murder?

The question was too bothersome; it had gone unanswered for too long. I made up my mind to come right out and ask. And I'd persist until I got an answer.

This was as good a time as any to start, I decided, as I pushed myself out of the chair. Pain shot up through my leg but I forced myself to ignore it, putting as little weight on it as possible as I hobbled out of the room, across the hall to Carlotta's door. I tapped softly.

'Yes?'

She was staring out the window. She didn't bother to turn around when I entered and closed the door behind me. When she finally did turn I saw a look on her face that told me she had expected someone else, not me.

'Jennifer,' she said, hurrying toward me. She put her arm around my waist.

171

'You mustn't be walking around. Here, sit down. You'll never get that sprain healed by putting weight on it.'

'I had to talk to you,' I said. I settled myself in a chair. Carlotta pulled another chair close to mine and sat down.

'What's bothering you? You look as though you've made up your mind to something.'

'I have. I thought you had better fill in some of the blank spaces.'

'I have no idea what you're talking about.'

'Philip just proposed.'

'Oh?' She sighed. 'But, of course, I am not surprised. The men here in Portugal are not exactly slow in going after what they want. They don't waste time. I assume you refused him?'

'No, I didn't refuse him. Why should I?'

'Jen!' She grabbed my hand. 'You mustn't marry Philip. You can't.'

'And why not? Please, Carlotta. You must tell me what's going on around here. I feel as though I'm living a nightmare of some kind. Tell me about Angelica. I want to know.'

Carlotta's eyes moved nervously toward the door. 'We can't talk here,' she said softly. 'If I fetch you a cane, do you think you can manage to make it downstairs? We'll go for a drive. I can't risk our being overheard.'

Between the cane and Carlotta, I managed the stairs. We got into Carlotta's car and started out toward her villa — the road that eventually led into the village. When we came to a wide section of the road, Carlotta pulled the car under a shade tree and switched off the motor.

She turned in the seat. 'What I have to say, Jen, is something I swore I would never tell a living soul. Unfortunately, you have become innocently involved in something that would ordinarily not concern you. But as you are involved, I suppose it is best that I keep my silence no longer.'

'Philip?'

She nodded. 'You must be told the truth so that you can make up your own mind about marrying him.'

'What truth?'

She took a deep breath and let it out

slowly. 'As you know, Neil was married to an American girl by the name of Angelica Scott.'

'I didn't know she was an American.'

'She was. And she was a very frivolous, spoiled girl. The marriage was not a very happy one, at least for Angelica. Neil, unfortunately, loved her very deeply. Angelica wasn't exactly true to Neil. She wasn't the type of girl to be true to any man. She was a high-spirited little thing, no more than nineteen years old. Neil was about twenty-five at the time. Philip was more the girl's age and closer to her in spirit, so it was natural that they spent a lot of time together. Neil didn't mind, really. He doesn't have a jealous bone in his body. He was teaching at Coimbra at the time and was away a lot.

'One night he returned to Alenquer Castle and found Angelica and his brother, Philip, in flagrante delicto, if you know what I mean. There was an ugly scene. Neil ordered his brother out of the house. Philip asked Angelica to come with him but Neil forbade it, threatening to divorce Angelica and cut Philip off without a red cent if they went away together. Neil has a terrible temper.

'Anyway, Angelica, defiant little thing that she was, laughed in her husband's face and told him to go ahead with the divorce, that she was going to run off with Philip regardless of what he threatened to do to them.' Again she paused. I thought I saw tears in her eyes but her head was slightly down and I couldn't be sure.

'While Philip was upstairs in his room packing,' she continued, 'he heard Neil and Angelica quarrelling horribly. He went down to try to do something to quiet them, but just as he entered the library he saw Neil pick up a poker and strike Angelica with it.'

'Oh, no,' I gasped. I was staring at her, my eyes wide with horror.

'Yes, he killed her,' Carlotta said, avoiding my eyes. 'He also tried to kill Philip. They fought and struggled and Neil, being the stronger, succeeded in hitting Philip, but luckily he only knocked him unconscious.'

'How awful.'

'Yes, it was. Anyway, when Philip regained

consciousness he found that Neil had carried Angelica out into the garden cottage and had set fire to it with Angelica and himself inside. The blaze was quite out of control by the time Philip reached it, but somehow he did manage to pull his brother to safety. Neil's face was scarred by a burning beam. The roof collapsed completely before Philip could get back in for Angelica.'

Carlotta's voice stayed even and calm, as though she were speaking through a trance. 'When Neil came to his senses, he begged Philip not to inform the police of his fight with Angelica. His wife was known to be a heavy smoker so they made up the story of her falling asleep with a cigarette. Neil had saved Philip's life when they were children aboard their parent's yacht. Philip felt he owed his life to Neil. Besides, Philip couldn't bring himself to have Neil sent to prison. He knew that Neil had always been a bit strange since the time he saw his parents perish in the fire. Neil isn't altogether right in the head, Jen. That yachting accident was no accident either — at least

Philip thinks it wasn't. Neil is what is generally known as a pyromaniac, I'm afraid. An arsonist, if you will. Philip told me he has always showed signs of it, even when they were children.'

I shook my head in disbelief. This was the man who had picked me up at the airport, the man I'd spent several hours with alone in a speeding car. But he'd been all right then, and he'd been all right when he had thought rationally enough to scare me away from the shark-infested waters of the ocean. And he'd carried me when I injured my ankle.

Yet this was the same man who had struck down his wife and had tried to kill his brother and had tried to burn himself alive beside his wife's body!

Carlotta sighed. 'I promised Philip I would never tell anyone about this, but I think you have a right to know.'

'Philip told you all this?'

She continued to smile. 'You remember my telling you several days ago that I once fell in love with the wrong man? That wrong man was Philip Alenquer.'

'Philip?' My mouth fell open.

'Yes, Philip. A man young enough to be my son. There's no fool like an old fool. Philip came to me very upset the night it happened. He stayed all night, talking, trying to decide what he should do. He loves his brother very much. He couldn't see him confined to any kind of institution. He made me promise never to tell anyone the true story of what happened that night. Loving him as much as I did, I agreed, of course. I would have agreed to anything Philip wanted in those days.'

'Then Neil must know that you know what happened that night.'

'He suspects, I'm afraid. It has never been discussed.'

'Poor Neil. Isn't there something that can be done for him? Treatments? Doctors?'

'He wouldn't permit any of it. Philip has tried but without success.'

We sat in silence for a while. Finally Carlotta roused herself and switched on the motor of the car. 'I can't advise you what to do about Philip's proposal, Jen. That's something you must decide for yourself.'

'I didn't know about you and Philip. I never suspected.'

'Naturally not,' she said as she steered the car back onto the road. 'I never advertised my love due to the vast difference in our ages. But don't let it make any difference, Jen. I admit I tend to be a little possessive of Philip. I'm still very fond of him. He doesn't love me; he never really did. He just came to me for the security and maturity I could offer him. If you have decided to marry him, then please don't concern yourself about me.'

'I didn't give Philip a definite answer,' I told her. 'I said I had to have time to think. I'm still not sure I'm completely over Andrew.'

'Then take your time, Jen. Don't rush into this mess until you're very sure. And don't let Philip rush things for you. Maybe we should take a little trip for a couple of weeks — go up to Paris, perhaps. It would give you time to think things out without Philip hovering around clouding your vision.' She laughed suddenly. 'Of course, if one has to have someone hovering around, Philip certainly is a very handsome hoverer.'

I found myself smiling along with her.

'Unfortunately,' Carlotta continued, 'We won't be able to get away from here for a couple of days. You have that sprained ankle, and I have to stick around and wait for the insurance people to finish their investigation of the fire. They made me promise to stay close where they could reach me.'

I suddenly thought of the fire and our nearly being burned alive. 'Was that Neil's doing?' I asked hesitantly.

'I try not to think of it, Jen, and I suggest you do the same. Neil's mind is deranged. He isn't responsible. It's a sickness, I'm afraid.'

'He'll have to have professional help.'

'That will come in time, dear,' she said as we rushed toward Alenquer Castle. 'And as far as you are concerned, you have nothing but time.'

Somehow or other I felt that wasn't entirely true. Time seemed to be running out for me, but I couldn't understand why.

13

The moon was still full. I was standing on the balcony looking up at it when Carlotta tapped on my door.

'You shouldn't put weight on that ankle,' she said when she saw me. 'You're not planning on going down to dinner? Theresa will fix you a tray.'

'No, I have this,' I said holding up my cane. 'And your arm. I'm not an invalid, Auntie, and I don't want to be treated as one. My ankle is fine. It scarcely hurts at all.'

'Nevertheless, I think you're being a bit hasty. But far be it from me to tell you what to do.'

I limped in from the balcony and seated myself in a chair. 'I told Philip that you and I were planning on going to Paris,' I said.

'What did he say?' She began toying with a large handkerchief she carried.

'I don't believe he liked it very much,

but I insisted I wanted time alone to think things out. He's very persuasive, as you know, but I didn't relent.'

'Good for you. I know just how persuasive that charming little dickens can be.' She looked misty-eyed as though remembering some fond old memory. I imagined she had a storehouse of those when it came to Philip. I could easily understand why Carlotta had fallen in love with him, a man so much younger than herself — a boy, actually. And I could see why Angelica had decided to run away with him. A man like Philip Alenquer was easy to love. He was gay and fun and extremely good-looking. His brother Neil, on the other hand, was quiet, moody, sensitive — like Andy Fuller.

Carlotta glanced at the tiny watch on her wrist. 'Well, if I'm going to help you hobble downstairs we'd best get going.' She hesitated. 'Are you absolutely sure you want to go downstairs for dinner?'

'I'm sure. I don't want to baby this ankle. Besides, I made it down those stairs earlier when we went for our drive.'

'You didn't say anything to Philip about what I told you, did you?' Carlotta asked, narrowing her eyes as she offered me her arm.

'Of course not. I'm a Carter, just like you,' I said. 'I am very good at keeping secrets.'

'I should have known better than to ask.' She squeezed my hand. 'I'm rather glad Philip proposed to you. It's a sure way of keeping you here in Portugal near me. I didn't like to think of your going back to Michigan.'

'I may still go back. I haven't definitely decided to marry Philip.'

Carlotta chuckled softly. 'I think you will,' she said. 'I think you'll be married within a month.'

We started down the stairs slowly, taking one step at a time. It was a little unwieldy with the cane in one hand and the other on the banister.

Everything happened so quickly. A figure darted somewhere behind us. Carlotta screamed as someone shoved her forward. I instinctively clutched at her to keep her from falling, only to be pulled off balance and pitched forward also. Her weight tore free of me. I screamed and grabbed the banister with both hands and held on.

Carlotta tumbled over and over and over, down the long, winding stairs. After what seemed an eternity, she came to rest at the very bottom, her body sprawled grotesquely on the marble floor. Her head lolled to one side; her eyes were closed; her limbs jutted from her torso at awkward angles. One leg was beneath her.

I clung to the banister, staring down at Carlotta's twisted body, my mind reeling. The last thing I felt before the blackness consumed me was hands steadying me. Someone swept me up into his arms, shouting.

When I opened my eyes I was lying on a sofa in the salon. Theresa was rubbing my wrists and there was a cold cloth on my forehead. We were alone in the room.

Consciousness came back in a sickening flash. I sat up quickly, my hands clutching my throat. 'Carlotta!' I screamed.

'No, no, senhorita. Lie still. Senhor Philip and Senhor Neil are looking after the senhora. She had a very bad fall. We have called for an ambulance.'

I sat there, dazed out of my mind. Nothing was registering except the vivid memory of Aunt Carlotta tumbling over and over down the long, winding stairs. My stomach contracted; I felt desperately sick with fear. The tears came in a rush. What was happening to us? I felt I was living a nightmare. At every turn something evil and cruel seemed to leap out at me.

Arms went around me. I felt my face pressed against someone's cheek — a masculine cheek. Through my watery eyes I saw a jagged scar, wet and glistening with my tears. I pushed myself away and stared up into Neil's face.

'It's all right, Jennifer. It's all right,' he said softly. 'Your aunt is hurt but it was not a fatal fall. She has regained consciousness. Philip is making her as comfortable as possible until the ambulance arrives.'

As if on cue, the squealing sound of a siren pierced the night air. Headlights streaked passed the tall paneled windows.

Men's voices. Hurrying footsteps. I found myself clutching tight to Neil.

Somewhere inside my head a spark ignited into a flame. My reason blazed like a beacon. Everything came back to me in a rush. The stairs, the fall, the fleeting dark figure that shoved Carlotta off balance, pitching her forward, dragging me with her. Our motor trip — Carlotta's information about Angelica's death — it all came back to me.

I shoved Neil away with all the strength and ran out of the salon. The pain in my ankle was excruciating, but I didn't care.

'Carlotta!' I yelled.

In the foyer I stopped dead. Men in white were easing Carlotta's limp body onto a stretcher.

'Carlotta,' I cried, trying to throw myself on her body. Hands restrained me.

'She is hurt, Jennifer,' Philip said as he pulled me away. 'There are several broken bones. You had best let the doctors examine her. Come away. They will take her to the hospital here for tonight. Tomorrow we will have her transferred to Lisboa if the doctors think it right.'

'Jennifer,' a low, strangled voice murmured. Carlotta turned her head on the stretcher and tried to hold out her hand. 'Go away from here, Jennifer,' Carlotta groaned. 'Go away from this place. Run, run away.' Her eyes closed and she slipped into unconsciousness.

I stood staring as they carried her out. No one stirred. We all were frozen in our various attitudes. Again the jarring sound of the siren repeated itself. Again the headlights swept across the windows as the ambulance sped away down the drive.

'Come into the salon,' Philip said, easing me back toward the room where Theresa and Neil remained motionless in the doorway. 'A brandy will help calm you.'

Neil's eyes met mine.

'No,' I said harshly. 'No, leave me alone. Please leave me alone.' I squirmed away from him and ran limping headlong up the long, twisting stairway that had almost brought about Carlotta's death as well as my own. My ankle ached. I hobbled, I stumbled, but I ran for my life. I shoved myself into my room, banged closed the door and threw myself across the bed.

I cried and cried and cried.

Sometime later I heard Theresa come silently into the room. She carried a tray. Placing it on the night table, she seated herself beside me on the bed.

'I have forbidden the senhors to come near you,' she said kindly. 'I have brought you something to eat. Try, senhorita. Try a little broth or some milk. You must eat something. It will help.'

Her kindly voice and her gentleness stemmed my tears. I pushed myself up off the bed and sat beside her. Theresa fumbled into the pocket of her skirt and handed me a handkerchief. It was scented very delicately with lilac.

'We do not know how this could have happened,' Theresa said.

I blotted my eyes and blew my nose softly. I turned and gave her a cold, calculating look. 'I know very well how it happened,' I said icily.

'The senhora — she tripped.'

'She didn't trip, Theresa. She was pushed down those stairs. Someone tried

188

to push both of us to our deaths.'

Theresa's eyes widened with horror. 'No. It cannot be. You are imagining.'

My anger was too intense to bother with polite civility. 'I did *not* imagine anything. I suppose you want me to think I imagined it, just as everyone wants me to think I imagined the blazing fire in the garden and the man who hovered over me here in my bedroom. But I did *not* imagine it, Theresa, and don't tell me I did. We were shoved off balance at the top of that staircase. Someone wanted us to die.'

Poor Theresa simply sat there staring at me as though I had suddenly turned into a raving lunatic.

I forced myself to be calm. I was being foolish to spend my anger on Theresa. I touched her arm and squeezed it tenderly. 'No, it is I who am sorry, Theresa. Forgive me. I am not being myself. I'm very upset, I'm afraid.'

'Yes, of course you are, senhorita. Come eat a bit and then rest. You have done damage enough to your swollen ankle I am afraid.'

I'd almost forgotten my ankle. It seemed a minute injury compared with what Carlotta had suffered.

'I will bring you your cane,' Theresa said, getting up from the bed. 'Please, senhorita, try to take a little broth.' She motioned toward the dinner tray. 'Eat and then rest. The senhors are both at the hospital with your aunt. No one will disturb you, so rest yourself.'

My mind wasn't on either food or rest. Eating was the last thing I wanted to do, yet unconsciously I undraped the tray and idly spooned broth into my mouth.

Theresa came in with my cane. She smiled when she saw me sipping the glass of warm milk. She didn't say anything. She merely put the cane within reaching distance and withdrew.

I should go to Carlotta, I told myself. Carlotta. I suddenly remembered Carlotta's words. She told me to get out of Alenquer Castle. She said I must get away. She didn't want me here alone. She warned me to run away.

Run away . . . run away . . . The words resounded inside my head.

The glass seemed to get heavier in my hand. At the same time my head started to get lighter and lighter. The room began to whirl around. I couldn't take my eyes from the empty milk glass I held. I tried to set it on the tray but my eyes wouldn't focus. The glass dropped to the floor and rolled away.

I felt drowsy — very drowsy. My eyelids were weighted down. I tried to get up. I wanted to go to Carlotta. I reached for the cane. It skidded away from my touch. It fell to the floor. I stooped over to retrieve it.

Once again darkness took control of me.

14

The tray was gone from the night table when I awoke. Sun was streaming in through the windows. I felt groggy and my head ached slightly.

I knew I'd been drugged and the thought made me more angry than afraid. I had to get away from Alenquer Castle. My mind settled on that objective and nothing else. I would go to Carlotta. I would dress quickly and quietly and slip away before anyone realized it. Carlotta would tell me what to do. I had to get to her. I had to find her.

I threw back the covers, suddenly noticing that I was wearing a nightdress. Theresa must have come in during the night, removed the tray and undressed me. The idea disturbed me. Anything could have befallen me in my drugged state. What kind of a household was this, anyway? Putting sleeping draughts in one's milk was not what I considered ethical. Surely Philip hadn't had a hand in it.

Someone tapped lightly on the door. Quickly I got back into bed and covered myself. I pretended to be sleeping. Whoever came in to check on me came no further than the foot of the bed. I waited, holding my breath. The scent of lilacs drifted past my nostrils. Theresa was there looking at me.

Then I heard her move away and the door close softly. I waited. After a while I slowly raised my lids. The room was empty. I hopped out of bed, picked up the cane and hobbled to the door. I heard nothing, no movement, no sounds. I eased the bolt shut. I couldn't chance being discovered dressing and packing my few belongings.

I ignored the throbbing in my head as I tossed articles helter-skelter into a small suitcase. I brushed my hair, made myself as presentable as possible, clicked shut the suitcase and started to leave. Carefully I slid back the bolt and opened the door a crack. The hallway was empty. A glance at my watch told me it was late morning, so everyone would undoubtedly be up and around.

I went across the hall into Carlotta's room. Quickly I rummaged in her handbag and found the keys to her car. I pressed them tightly into my palm and left, picking up my suitcase as I went back out into the hall.

At the top of the stairs I hesitated. The horror of last night returned. The steps stretched out below me; they seemed treacherous and unsafe. They looked as though they were moving — swaying, tilting as I stood looking down at them. I pressed my back hard against the wall and, supporting myself with my cane, slid down one step at a time. I moved slowly, cautiously.

Halfway down I heard voices. A door opened and closed. I pressed myself against the wall and held my breath. Theresa and Neil came from the back of the house. I sat down on the stairs and cowered against the wall, trying to make myself as inconspicuous as possible.

They spoke in Portuguese. Theresa asked a question. The only words I understood were 'Senhor Philip.' They were directly below me in the foyer. I saw Neil shrug his shoulders and answer something. I didn't understand.

My luck held. Theresa went toward the salon. Neil went directly out through the front door with not so much as a glance in the direction of the staircase. I waited for the door to close behind him. Then, keeping my eyes firmly fixed on the doorway of the salon, I inched my way down the stairs, one step at a time. I could see Theresa bending, moving around as she dusted and straightened. She was too intent upon her work to notice me moving to the bottom of the stairs and starting toward the front door.

I hurried as best I could, hoping against hope that my cane would not make a noise. I reached the front door and stood there for a moment. My heart was pounding; my hand felt hot and clammy on the knob. Neil was somewhere outside, I knew. Theresa would be coming back into the foyer at any minute. I had to get away. I had to get out of there before they discovered me.

I eased open the front door, and seeing no sign of Neil, slipped outside. I stood under the portico, concealing myself as best I could among the ornately carved pillars that supported the roof. Staying in the shadows as much as possible, I moved slowly through the bushes, skirted the side of the castle and started to where I knew Carlotta's car was parked.

As I rounded the corner I stopped dead in my tracks. I pulled back, pressing myself hard against the side of the castle. Neil was immediately around the corner, polishing the limousine. My heart sank. Directly next to the limousine was Carlotta's roadster.

I crouched behind some bushes and tried to devise a plan. I made up my mind to hide in the bushes until the way was clear, even if it took forever. I heard a window creaking open somewhere overhead. I heard Theresa call Neil in a loud anxious voice. She yelled down something to him. I heard 'senhorita' in whatever it was she was yelling and knew she'd found my room empty.

Neil ran past the bush behind which I

was hiding and into the house. I lost no time. I hobbled as quickly as I could toward Carlotta's car. The keys were digging into my hand. I threw my case on the back seat, tossed the cane on the front seat and slipped behind the wheel. My hand was shaking badly as I tried to fit the key into the ignition. I pushed in on the clutch and moved the gear shift to neutral. My ankle pained as I held in the clutch and twisted the key. I jammed my foot down on the accelerator and the car roared to life, sending a jet of exhaust out from behind. Quickly I released the brake and rammed the gear shift into reverse, backing the car out of the garage. Just as I turned the wheel and pushed the gear shift into forward I saw Neil come out the front door. He was waving his hands at me and calling my name.

The car lurched forward. I held my foot securely down on the accelerator and raced toward him. He was standing directly in the middle of the drive. He didn't move.

'Jennifer! No! Wait!'

I fixed my eyes firmly ahead. The car

bore directly down on Neil. I had to get away. Neil stayed in the middle of the drive. I twisted the wheel and swung the car into a clump of bushes, gunned the motor and swerved around him. He made a lunge at the car but I pressed down on the accelerator and sped off, leaving Neil reeling in the billowing dust. In the rear-view mirror I saw him regain his balance, turn and run as fast as he could toward the limousine.

I didn't use the brakes at the turn of the gate. The car swung wide, its back tires skimming over the gravel road as I fought to control the wheel. I glanced in the rear-view mirror again and saw Neil's limousine race out of the driveway and make the turn onto the road. It streaked toward me. I shoved my foot down on the gas pedal as far as it would go and braced myself against the curving, twisting, turning road.

Neil's car was gaining on me. He was used to this road whereas I fought every curve, every turn. Dust billowed out from behind the car as I swerved and spun and tried to keep from going off the road.

Through the dust, Neil's car kept getting closer and closer. He was a far more expert driver than I and I knew I would have to throw caution to the winds if I intended to escape him.

Carlotta's car seemed to be fighting me. It groaned and creaked as I pushed it faster and faster. Up ahead I saw the road cut sharply to the right. I braced myself for the curve. I eased up just slightly on the accelerator, groping for the feel of the curve.

The turn was too sharp. I slammed my foot down on the brake pedal. The pedal went right to the floor. I panicked. I pumped and pumped on the brake, but the car refused to slow down. I skidded around the sharp curve, tires squealing, motor racing; the back wheels slid sideways over the gravel; the car almost turned over. It righted itself, miraculously, and I managed somehow to get it back into the center of the road. I pushed on.

Perspiration beaded my forehead. My teeth bit into my lower lip as I struggled with the car. A glance in the mirror told me I hadn't lost Neil. He was still gaining on me.

The road straightened out. For miles ahead it lay like a straight, unbroken ribbon. I refused to think of the brakes. If worse came to worst I could use the emergency brake. I coaxed the car faster and faster, but it was no use — Neil was directly behind me. He was starting to pull up next to me, the hood of his car even with the back of mine. He inched forward. I cut to the right and tried to squeeze him onto the shoulder. The fenders crunched together. I heard Neil yell something, but I blocked my ears and kept my foot jammed down on the gas pedal. Neil's car fell back a few feet. Then he started to gain on me again.

Again he got even with my car and again I cut sharply toward him. His car lurched onto the shoulder. I saw him struggle with the wheel. I was sure he was going into the ditch but at the last possible second he yanked at the wheel and bounced back onto the road.

This time when he pulled up next to me it was he who cut his car sharply into me. I braced myself, gripping the wheel as tightly as I could. He inched his car over. The front fenders touched. I heard the scraping of metal.

He eased me over, over, over onto the soft shoulder, off into the bushes and trees that edged the side of the road. Carlotta's car bounced and thumped. A huge rock lay hidden in the midst of a clump of bushes. I didn't see it in time. I tried to pull back onto the road but it was too late. The rock tore at the underside of the car. With a sickening jolt the car came to a dead stop. My head banged against the steering wheel, stunning me. I sat there listening to the pounding in my head, the rush of the blood through my veins, the hammering of my heart.

'You little fool,' Neil yelled as he ran back to me. 'What were you trying to do?'

'Don't touch me. Let me go,' I yelled, forcing my senses back into focus.

Neil reached for the door handle. I pounded my fists against his hand, his arms. 'Get away from me!' I yelled, half-hysterical with fear. 'Get away. Let me go. Let me go.'

He yanked open the door and reached for me. I fought him with all the strength I had. He pulled me from behind the wheel. I kicked, I scratched, I clawed at him but he held me tight against his chest.

'Put me down! Let me go!' I yelled, still pounding, kicking, pummeling him. I yelled the first thing that came into my head. 'Murderer — murderer — murderer.'

His face was a mask. He carried me toward the limousine, then put me down on my feet. I felt the strength go out of his body. The moment I touched the ground my hand slashed out and I slapped him hard across the face. His lack of response, the sadness in his eyes froze my hand before I could slap him again. He just stood there looking down at me. There was no hatred, no intent to kill. He was looking at me — stunned. His expression was blank, his eyes dead.

'Get in the car,' he said evenly. He spoke so quietly, so calmly that I almost didn't hear him. 'I will drive you into the village.' He turned and walked away from me. He rounded the car and got behind the wheel. He reached across the seat and opened the door nearest me. 'Get in, Jennifer,' he said again. 'Please. I mean you no harm.'

I couldn't bring myself to trust him. I stood there trying to think what I should do. I was trapped. There was no escape now. If I got into the car I knew he would turn around and take me back to Alenquer Castle — I knew he would.

I squared my shoulders and pushed myself away from the bruised fender of the old limousine. Like someone in a trance, I walked, limping, back to Carlotta's car. I slid in behind the wheel and sat there, staring straight ahead at nothing. If he were going to take me back it would have to be by physical force.

Out of the corner of my eye I saw Neil get out of the limousine and start toward me. I braced myself, prepared to fight him with every ounce of strength I had left in my body. But he did nothing. He came over and stood beside the car. I thought for a moment that he was surveying the damage to the automobile.

He wasn't — he was surveying me.

'Why are you so afraid of me?' he asked softly. 'Why do you call me a murderer? What have I done?'

I turned and looked up into his face, but the moment I saw his eyes, soft and hurt, my coldness melted. I felt a thickening in my throat. The stinging behind my lids returned and I buried my face in my hands and started to cry.

I felt his touch. It was gentle and yet strong. I pulled away.

'Your aunt has put wrong notions in your head, I think,' he said. 'For that I am sorry. I do not want you to hate me. I am no murderer. I killed no one.'

'You almost killed me,' I shouted through my tears. I was on the verge of hysteria again. I felt it creeping up all over me.

'I was only trying to stop you. Your aunt told me yesterday the brakes went out on her car.'

'I would have managed,' I said stubbornly.

He said nothing for a moment. 'I was merely trying to help. And besides, there are some things I wanted to say to you.'

'There is nothing you and I have to say to each other.'

'There is Philip.'

He said it so casually, my head snapped around and I stared at him. 'Philip and I are not your business,' I snapped.

His expression stayed blank. 'But you are both my business,' he insisted.

I groped in my pocket for a handkerchief. He held one out to me. It was the same handkerchief he'd given me once before — the one I'd kicked under the chair on the terrace — the one I knew now had belonged to Angelica. I ignored it. I pulled my own handkerchief from my pocket and wiped my eyes.

'I do not blame you for being afraid of me,' he said as he carefully refolded Angelica's handkerchief and tucked it into his pocket again. 'My face is not very handsome.'

I unconsciously glanced at the ugly scar on his left cheek. I said nothing. I turned and continued to blot my eyes, gradually getting my heart back to normal. I suddenly wasn't half as frightened as I had been moments before. Instinctively, I had the feeling that nothing terrible would come to me now.

'It isn't your scar that frightens me,' I managed to say after a short interval of silence.

'What then? Perhaps it is your aunt's gossip, yes?'

I bit down on my lower lip. It felt sore. Then I remembered the harrowing drive down the twisting road. I said nothing.

Neil stood there for a moment waiting for my response. When it didn't come he said, 'You must not marry my brother, Jennifer. It would be a terrible mistake.'

I suddenly remembered what Philip had said about Neil wanting to take everything from him. 'I don't think it is a mistake.'

'You do not know him at all. You only met him a few days ago. How can you be so sure you want to marry him?'

'I'm not sure,' I blurted out, having been caught off guard. I saw his eyebrows arch upward when I glanced at him. 'Carlotta and I were planning to go away for a while until I made up my mind.'

'I did not know that. I am glad to hear

it,' Neil answered. 'You are more sensible than I gave you credit for being.'

'However,' I continued spitefully, 'I don't think my absence from Philip will make the least bit of difference. I love him.' *That isn't true*, a little voice said inside my head. *At least, you aren't absolutely sure, Jennifer.* But when I looked at the shocked expression on Neil's face, I felt determined to let the remark stand.

'You cannot love him. You do not know him. You are being childish.'

'How dare you interfere?'

'Because I must interfere. I do not want you hurt.'

I found words tumbling out of my mouth before realizing what they were. 'You can't be rid of me as easily and as cleverly as you got rid of Angelica,' I said. But the moment I heard the words I gasped and covered my mouth with my hand.

Again he stared at me. His eyes were needle-sharp. He narrowed them. 'What have people been telling you?' he demanded. His fists were suddenly clenched so tightly the knuckles were white.

I couldn't speak.

'I demand that you tell me. What have you been told about Angelica? Do you think that I destroyed her? Do you think that?' His voice was raised. There was a slight tremor in it.

I refused to let him browbeat me. 'Didn't you?'

I thought for a moment he was going to strike me. I cringed away from him. Then I saw his shoulders sag, his head droop. He looked down at the ground for a long time. When he raised his head and looked at me I saw his eyes were moist. 'Who told you such a thing? Carlotta? Philip?'

Again I couldn't answer him.

'Your aunt has been most unkind, if it was she. If it was Philip, then I understand.'

I tried to squirm out of my uncomfortable situation. 'Carlotta felt I should know before giving Philip's proposal serious consideration.'

'Know what?'

I was making a terrible botch of things, but I was in too deep now to turn back.

'She told me the truth about Angelica's death,' I said.

'The truth? What truth?'

I couldn't look at him. Everything was going all wrong. I didn't know what to say, where to turn. I couldn't bring myself to confront him with the fact that I'd been told he killed his wife. I started to tremble.

'Please, Neil,' I said, trying not to show the terror I suddenly felt again. 'Don't press me. What happened between you and your wife is no concern of mine. Carlotta only meant to help me. She didn't think I should marry Philip until I knew what I was letting myself in for by becoming an Alenquer.'

'You think I murdered Angelica?'

'I don't want to talk about it.'

He closed his eyes. His fists were still clenched tightly together but he forced himself to relax. He leveled his gaze on me, looking like a man who had just suffered the most bitter of defeats. 'Come along, Jennifer,' he said. 'I will not bother you any more. Come. I will drive you to your aunt.'

I didn't move. I couldn't.

'You cannot stay here,' he said.

I squared my shoulders and jutted out my chin. 'But I intend to,' I told him.

He let out an exasperated sigh. I saw him fighting with his conscience. The scar on the side of his face seemed to glow bright red. It throbbed and pulsed, but for some odd reason it did not repulse me.

'I did not kill Angelica,' he said flatly. 'Philip did.'

15

My head came up. My eyes widened with disbelief. 'You're lying,' I gasped.

'No, I am not lying,' he said, again looking to the ground, avoiding my eyes. Then slowly his eyes raised and met mine. 'I do not lie,' he said, staring me straight in the face. 'I did not think I would ever tell that to a living soul.'

I couldn't believe him. I told him so.

'It is the truth,' he said with a shrug. He looked resigned, almost relieved. He impressed me as a man who had suddenly lost a heavy burden — one he'd been carrying for a long, long time.

'You're only saying that to turn me against Philip.'

'I admit I am trying to turn you against my brother, but I am not telling you a lie. I do not like saying what I am saying, but I cannot protect Philip any longer. Things are becoming too dangerous. Philip gets worse and worse with each passing day.

After what he attempted last night I am only too well aware of his potential for evil. I had to lock him in his room so that he wouldn't harm you further. I know that he will do you serious harm one day and he will not be aware of what he is doing. His mind is not sound, Jennifer. He is a sick man, a very sick man.'

I wouldn't believe what he was saying. 'Why would Philip kill Angelica?'

'She refused to run away with him. They quarreled.'

'No. You and Angelica quarreled.'

He shook his head. 'Angelica and Philip quarreled. I threatened to divorce Angelica. I told Philip I would cut him off without a penny. Angelica said she would stay with me. She was too accustomed to luxury, wealth. She did not want to take the chance that I would make good my threat. She was not the type of woman who would be happy in poverty. She had to have money and a position. She chose to stay with me.'

'And knowing how Angelica felt about Philip, you didn't care? You still wanted her to remain your wife?'

'I was much younger then. I thought I loved her more than life itself. Philip flew into a rage and struck Angelica. I rushed to my wife's side and Philip knocked me unconscious with a poker. When I came to, the cottage in the grove was on fire and Angelica was lying inside. Philip was standing outside laughing — laughing up at the full moon. I tried to get Angelica out, but I was too late. The roof collapsed.' He touched the scar on his cheek. His eyes weren't on me. He was seeing a scene many, many years old.

I shook my head. 'And why did you not tell this story to the authorities?'

'Angelica was dead. I saw no reason to have two deaths on my conscience. If I had not made a scene, if I had not threatened, if I had given Angelica up, none of it would have happened.' He paused, reflecting. 'No, I suppose it was inevitable,' he said finally. 'Philip was always a bit mentally unstable.'

'Isn't it strange,' I said. 'Philip made the same remark about you.'

Neil was taken aback. 'Philip told you that I — ' He didn't finish the sentence.

'But ask Theresa,' he said. 'She was there. She knows everything.'

Now it was my turn to be taken aback. 'Theresa?'

'Yes. She saw and heard everything that night. She knows about my brother's pyromania. It was Philip who set fire to our parents' yacht. It is the full moon. It affects him in terrible ways.'

'That's nonsense.'

'It is not nonsense. The full moon causes some people to do strange things. The actions and behavior of many are influenced by the full moon. Please, Jennifer. If you do not wish to believe me, at least speak with Theresa. I will tell her to tell you everything.'

My mind was in a flurry of confusion. Of course he would tell Theresa to tell me everything, I thought. Theresa would most likely say just about anything Neil wanted her to say. No, I would believe Carlotta above everyone else. And I would believe Philip. I could not bring myself to believe this terrifying man with the dark, sad eyes and the scarred cheek. I didn't want to believe him.

Somewhere in the distance I heard the sound of an approaching car. Neil heard it also. He turned his head and listened. He turned back and studied me for a time, then walked out into the center of the road. A battered pick-up truck was lumbering toward Alenquer Castle. Neil waved it down. The man behind the wheel wore a uniform. Neil and he conversed in Portuguese. I saw the man hand Neil some mail. Then the man smiled in my direction.

'I will take you into the village, senhorita,' he said in broken English.

'Go ahead, Jennifer,' Neil said. 'The postman will take you to your aunt if you do not feel you are safe with me. Go ahead. I will not force you to stay here.'

It was over, I thought with relief. I was free to go. Quickly I got my suitcase out of the back seat. I slid out from behind the wheel, took up my cane and limped toward the mail truck without so much as a glance at Neil. I could feel his eyes on me. I couldn't look at him.

I got into the cab of the truck with a little effort and seated myself next to the postman, placing my suitcase at my feet. Neil didn't make a move to help me. The driver backed the truck around and headed opposite to his original direction. We started down the road, leaving Neil standing there looking after us.

The man chatted away half in Portuguese, half in English. I nodded occasionally and smiled a lot, but I didn't understand what he was saying. Truthfully, I didn't hear much of it; my mind was completely taken up with the conflicting stories I'd heard from Carlotta and Neil. Of course I knew Carlotta's was the true story; Neil was only trying to keep me from marrying Philip.

But why? That was the major question in my mind. Why was Neil so against my marrying his brother? I couldn't flatter myself by giving any credence to Philip's explanation — that Neil was in love with me. That seemed utterly preposterous. There had to be another reason.

But perhaps Neil didn't have a reason. Perhaps he was simply being selfish and didn't want outsiders living at Alenquer Castle for fear they'd discover the truth about Angelica's death. Perhaps he felt his secret was safe only if he and Philip and Theresa knew about it. Why, then, had he told me?

I was so absorbed in my thoughts I wasn't even conscious of the fact that the postman had stopped chattering and had pulled up in front of a low, white building with a red cross insignia over the door. He said something and pointed.

I pushed my troubled thoughts out of my head for a second, smiled at him, picked up my bag and cane and hobbled down from the truck. I thanked him. He waved and drove off.

A nurse took me to Carlotta, who was in a small room at the far end of the corridor. Her leg was in a plaster cast and raised halfway up from the bed. One arm was also in a cast; the other lay limply at her side. Her head was bandaged. Her eyes were closed. Carlotta opened her eyes when the nurse touched her gently.

'Jennifer,' she said, trying to smile. 'Oh, baby, I'm so sorry.'

'There, there, auntie,' I said, rushing to her and kissing her cheek. 'Don't excite yourself. I'm all right. I'm here now. Everything is all right.'

'Some vacation I'm showing you, huh?' she said, again trying to smile.

'Don't try to talk.'

'Nonsense,' she said weakly. 'I'm all right, except for a few broken bones here and there.'

'Five, to be precise,' the nurse put in as she straightened the covers on the bed. 'She will be fine, senhorita, but she will be in bed for a long time.'

'I'll be out of here in a week,' Carlotta huffed.

The nurse gave her a stern look. 'You will do no such thing, Senhorita Carter. You will stay in that bed and you will behave yourself.'

Carlotta gave me a helpless look. 'You can't call your body your own in this flea bag.'

'Flea bag, indeed,' the nurse said with a grin, aping the American idiom. 'Wait until you receive our bill. You will not think it a flea bag then.'

Carlotta tried to laugh. Her laugh only caused her to start coughing. The nurse soothed her and eased her back against the pillows. She looked toward me. 'You can visit for as long as you like, senhorita. But try not to excite her or upset her or make her talk too much. I will be back when I feel you should leave.'

'Thank you,' I said and the nurse left us.

'Well, this is a fine kettle of lampreys, isn't it?' Carlotta teased, trying to sound light and unconcerned. Her expression told me she felt otherwise.

'Don't talk,' I told her as I pulled up a chair and seated myself beside the bed. I still carried the cane; the nurse had taken custody of my suitcase.

'Have you seen Philip?' Carlotta asked.

I decided it would only upset her if I repeated what Neil had said to me, that he had locked Philip in his room last night. 'No, not this morning. I'm afraid I left the castle in quite a hurry.'

'How did you get here?'

'The mailman gave me a lift.'

Carlotta chuckled low in her throat. 'You American women. You sure have get-up-and-go.'

'We American women,' I corrected, smiling.

Again she chuckled softly. 'Well, get yourself a room at the inn down the street. It's not the Ritz but it's clean and comfortable. Tell them you're my niece. They'll take good care of you. They should. I own a half-interest in the dump. Ask for Senhor Alphonse. He'll see to it that you're comfortable.'

'Don't worry about me. I'll be all right.'

Carlotta suddenly frowned. 'I think you'd better go home,' she said.

'To Michigan? Not on your life. I'm staying here to take care of you.'

Carlotta was about to protest but the nurse suddenly interrupted us. 'Is it time already?' I asked.

She shook her head. 'No. It is just that there is a gentleman here to see Senhorita Carter.' She looked at Carlotta. 'Are you well enough to speak with the fire commissioner?' she asked Carlotta.

Carlotta tried to straighten up on her pillows. I placed a restraining hand gently on her shoulder. 'Yes, sure,' she said. 'Show him in.' She gave me an odd look, then relaxed.

The man we'd conferred with a few

Northampton Library NC4

Customer ID: *******4982

Items that you have renewed

Title: Fire on the moon
ID: 80003490630
Due: 08 October 2022

Title: Mushrooms and toadstools of Britain &
Europe
ID: 80002867902
Due: 08 October 2022

Total items: 2
Account balance: £0.00
17/09/2022 16:02
Issued: 2
Overdue: 0
Reservations: 0
Ready for collection: 0

Thank you for visiting Northampton Library. We
look forward to seeing you again.

days before came into the room. He went directly to Carlotta, took her hand — and touched it to his lips. 'I deeply regret this unfortunate accident,' he said. 'You are having a run of ill fortune, senhorita.' Then he shrugged. 'But of course it is the nights of the full moon. Strange things always happen during the nights when the moon is full.' The man turned and looked at me. 'Ah, Senhorita Carter. I am so very glad you are here too. I have some rather upsetting news.'

I wasn't sure I'd heard him correctly. He was so matter-of-fact in his announcement. But there was no doubt in my mind, he had definitely said 'upsetting news'.

The man shrugged at Carlotta. 'I am sorry to have to add to your discomfort, but unfortunately this latest development needs immediate attention.' He pulled some papers from a briefcase he carried. 'I called at the castle and was told of your fall and that you were here,' he explained. 'I am happy to hear that you are not staying with the Alenquers.' His eyes wandered over to me. 'Or are you?' he asked.

'No, my niece is staying at the inn,' Carlotta told him.

'Good. Good. What we have discovered is quite shocking and it involves the Alenquers. As I told you the other day, we found an empty tin of gasoline near your property. We found it on the road leading to Alenquer Castle. It took a while for our experts to identify the fingerprints on the can. They were badly smudged and difficult to recognize, but we were fortunate in obtaining one excellent print.' He looked over his shoulder to make sure we were completely alone. He saw that the door to the room was open. He walked over, checked the hallway outside, then closed the door firmly. 'Philip Alenquer's fingerprint was on the can of gasoline,' he said.

'You mean Neil Alenquer.' I jumped to my feet.

The commissioner shook his head. 'No, Philip — the younger brother.'

'Are you absolutely certain?' Carlotta asked, her eyes wide with astonishment.

'Absolutely. There is no doubt whatsoever. That is why I am glad you are not staying at the castle. It would only make things worse for you.'

Without showing us the papers he had extracted from his briefcase, he replaced them. 'I do not understand what is going on,' he continued. 'Of course this means that there will be a complete investigation of the fire. Accident is out of the question. The fire was deliberately set. Why, we do not know. But it was definitely not accidental.'

Neil's words came back to me in a flash. Neil had said that Philip had pyromaniacal tendencies. Philip had set the fire. Why? If I believed Neil, the answer to that question was all too clear. But I couldn't believe Neil. I couldn't believe that Philip wanted to cause Carlotta harm — to cause me harm.

I wouldn't believe it.

Yet if I thought about it, everything Neil had said seemed to make sense.

16

I was finding it more and more impossible to straighten things out in my mind. I paced back and forth in the snug little hotel room, but the more I paced, the more muddled everything became.

Even tiny, unimportant details cluttered up my brain — such as Carlotta's half-interest in this village inn. She hadn't mentioned it when we talked about moving here. A little thing like that made me start to see Carlotta in a completely different light. She wasn't the Aunt Carlotta who had come to Michigan to visit every couple of years. She wasn't the same Aunt Carlotta I thought to be so scatterbrained and irresponsible. When in America she acted flighty, carefree. Here on her so-called native soil she was a completely different person, filled with secrets, intrigue, romance.

Yet I loved her as much as ever, even though I was filled with doubts about her.

No, I didn't actually doubt her; it was just that I now had certain reservations about her.

Carlotta was as much a mystery to me as Philip's fingerprints on the gasoline can. But that could easily be explained, I told myself. If the can of gasoline had come from Alenquer Castle, it was reasonable to assume that Philip might well have handled it at one time or another. Simply because his print was found on the can did not necessarily mean that it was he who had set fire to Carlotta's villa.

Neil, of course, would accuse his brother because Neil had reason to accuse Philip. Blaming Philip would remove suspicion from him. Still, there was something about Neil that made me feel he was sincere about what he had told me. Of course, he may have told himself the lie so often that he now actually believed it. And, remembering Andrew Fuller, I had to admit that I wasn't very good at judging people, especially men.

Another thing in Neil's favor was that he had saved my life again. The brakes being faulty, I could easily have been killed on that road. I never did test the emergency brake; how could I know it would have saved me in an emergency? If Neil hadn't come speeding after me, forcing me to a safe stop . . . I hated to think what could have happened.

Where was Philip?

I didn't ponder that question long. The answer came almost immediately. He tapped on the door of my room. 'Jennifer,' he breathed, pulling me into his arms. He crushed his mouth to mine before I knew what was happening, then held me away from him and looked at me. His smile was infectious. 'Theresa told me you ran away. Why?'

'They drugged me, Philip,' I answered breathlessly. 'Theresa put something in my milk last night. I didn't think it was a very nice thing for her to do without telling me.'

He frowned. 'No, I agree,' he said. A dark shadow passed over his eyes.

'And after what happened on the stairs — after Carlotta warned me to run away — I had to get out of there, away from Neil, away from Theresa.'

'And me?' he asked lightly, teasingly.

'Carlotta told me everything. She told me about Neil and Angelica.'

Philip stiffened. He held me at arm's length. 'Carlotta told you?'

'Yes, everything.'

Philip scowled. 'He's in love with you.'

'Don't worry about Neil, Philip. He only tried to scare me. After we're married — '

Philip's face lit up like a little boy's at Christmas. 'Then you will marry me,' he said happily.

'Yes, Philip. I'll marry you.'

'Oh, my darling, I love you so.'

'And I love you,' I found myself saying, but my words sounded oddly unconvincing.

'Come,' he said, taking my hand and pulling me with him.

'Where are we going?'

'I want to celebrate. We will drive down to the Algarve. We will take the coast road and stop for lunch along the beach. I want to remember this day for the rest of my life. You are making me a very happy man, Jennifer — a very, very happy man.'

'No.' Neil was standing in the doorway. His eyes were narrowed at Philip.

'Go home, Philip,' he said ominously.

'Get out of our way, Neil,' Philip said, regaining his composure. 'You have no right interfering with my life.'

'I have every right, and you know it.'

Philip suddenly became nervous. He couldn't look at his brother. 'I told Philip I'd marry him,' I said brazenly.

Neil took a step backward. His eyes widened. 'I thought you were planning to wait,' he said, his voice softening when he spoke to me.

'I've changed my mind.' I was determined to defy him, to stare him down. I lost. I found myself turning to Philip and leaning on him for support.

'You're a fool,' Neil said. 'I will not permit this marriage.'

'Now see here,' Philip started, tightening his arm around me. 'You will not interfere, Neil. I will not tolerate it. We are both of legal age. We will do as we wish. We do not need your consent or your blessing.'

'Go home, Philip,' Neil repeated, his

voice filled with fury. 'I will deal with you later.'

All the strength I had felt in Philip earlier suddenly drained from his body. I felt him go weak. His arm slipped from around my waist. He hung his head. I grabbed his hand and squeezed hard. For a moment he stood there, taking strength from me, then raised his head and jutted out his chin. 'No,' he said firmly.

Neil, however, merely spoke his name more harshly and when Philip finally turned to me, his eyes were pale and weak. He gave me a pleading look, patted my cheek and said, 'I will talk with you later.'

'Philip, wait . . . '

'Later,' Philip insisted, kissing me lightly on the mouth. He looked at Neil and his eyes filled with hatred. I thought he might strike him. He didn't. He merely stepped around Neil and left us there in the doorway.

I watched Philip go down the hall and disappear down the stairs. When he was gone I whirled on Neil. 'How dare you?' I said. 'You have no right.'

Neil didn't say anything for a moment. He propelled me back into my room and closed the door. 'I have every right,' he said. 'I told you that once before. You will not marry my brother.'

'You can't stop me,' I said, glowering at him.

'Perhaps not,' he said, 'But I intend to try. I told you on the road. You chose not to believe me, but I was telling you the truth and Philip knows the truth. That is why he will not stand up to me. He knows the harm I can do him.'

'You're a fiend.'

Before I knew what was happening he grabbed me and pulled me against him. He forced my head back. His mouth closed over mine. Time suddenly did not exist. The only thing that was real to me was Neil's body against mine. Neil's fingers stroked my hair as I hung in his arms.

'You do not love Philip,' he said cruelly. 'You are only using him as a replacement for your American lover.'

I heard the door slam.

Neil was gone.

17

'There is a telephone call for you, senhorita,' Senhor Alphonse told me when I answered his knock. I had half-expected to find Philip standing there. 'It is Senhor Alenquer. He said it was very important he talk to you.'

'Which Senhor Alenquer?' I asked, feeling my heart begin to pound.

The proprietor merely shrugged his shoulders. 'He did not say, senhorita.'

It had to be Philip. Neil wouldn't be calling me for any reason, I thought. Yes, it had to be Philip.

And it was.

'Darling,' he said, whispering so softly I could hardly hear him.

'Philip. What is it?'

'I cannot talk,' he said in a rush. 'Neil will be returning at any moment. You must help me.'

'Yes, of course, darling,' I said anxiously. 'What can I do?'

'They will lock me in my room again tonight,' he whispered. His voice sounded so strange I hardly recognized it. 'I can't get out unless you help me.'

Part of me wanted to say no, but I couldn't refuse his plea. 'Yes. Yes, I'll come. When? How?'

'I left my car in the garage at the inn. The keys are in the ignition. It's only six o'clock now. Neil and Theresa will retire about ten. Come about eleven. Take my car and park it near the gates. Do not bring the car up the drive. The keys to my room should be outside in the hall on the table. Do you think you can manage?'

'I'll manage, darling. Don't worry. And I'll be careful.'

'I will be waiting for you,' he whispered. The connection was severed. I stood there, holding the phone in my hand.

'Is everything all right, senhorita?' Senhor Alphonse inquired.

'Yes. Fine. Everything is fine,' I told him. I started back to my room but after a few steps I stopped and turned back to Senhor Alphonse. 'Did Senhor Philip

232

Alenquer leave his car in your garage this afternoon?'

'*Si*, senhorita. His car is here. He said he was leaving it for you to use.'

* * *

Dinner was served late at the inn. It was a simple affair, something Senhor Alphonse called *Bacalhau a Gomes de Sa*, a Portuguese dish with cod, potatoes and onions, garnished with eggs, olives and parsley.

I lingered over the excellent coffee and decided I had to see Carlotta. I hadn't wanted to upset her with current developments. I knew she would be against a hasty marriage to Philip. I dreaded telling her, but I'd made up my mind to marry Philip.

A stray thought crossed my mind. Was I marrying Philip out of spite? I shook my head. No, of course not; I loved Philip, I told myself. But the little voice inside my brain persisted: *How can you love a man you've known only a week?* I refused to listen.

I felt uncomfortable at the memory of Neil's kiss. I couldn't understand why I had reacted as I did. Neil had overpowered me, stolen my senses away. I hated myself for having given in to him. And I hated him more than ever.

At the hospital the nurse informed me that I wouldn't be able to visit Carlotta. 'You cannot see her now, senhorita. We have given her a sedative and she is sleeping. You will have to return in the morning.'

It was a beautiful night. The moon was still full, although it was beginning to wane. Its edges looked a bit less definite, less brilliant than on previous nights. The last night of the full moon, I said to myself as I looked up at it. I'd be starting a whole new life tomorrow with a whole new moon.

Back in my hotel room I tried to read, but my mind wasn't on anything except the hands of my watch. They seemed to creep from numeral to numeral. At ten o'clock I found I had to get out of the room. I couldn't sit still any longer.

I went down to the garage and found

Philip's car waiting for me. Everything was as he had said — the car was there, the keys in the ignition. I asked the man on duty to help me put down the convertible top. I wanted to be part of the night that surrounded me.

I drove slowly, carefully toward Alenquer Castle. I didn't feel the least bit nervous until I started to pass the gates of Carlotta's burned-out villa. For some reason my heart beat a little faster and my pulse pounded more loudly at my temples.

I had ample time. I decided to stop. Why? I didn't know. It was just that I had to kill time and felt that Carlotta's villa was as good a place as any to try to calm my sudden nervousness. Besides, while I was here, I thought, perhaps I might collect a few more of my belongings.

The villa was solidly boarded. The moon streamed down on its smoke-streaked facade, its toppled statuary and potted cypresses. I sat there, gazing at the once beautiful house. It would be beautiful again, I knew, and I suddenly longed for that beauty. I turned off the motor and switched off the headlights. I sat there debating with myself as to how I'd gain access. I could use a few more dresses, another light coat. But just how was I going to manage to get inside now that it was boarded up?

A snapping of a twig, a rustle of movement pushed the question out of my head. I clicked the headlights back on and peered into the darkness. Philip emerged from the woods, into the beams of the headlights.

'Philip,' I called with surprise when I recognized him.

He said nothing.

I pushed down on the door handle and started out of the car. Just then another pair of headlights swept the drive. I turned and saw Neil's limousine coming toward me. I shot a hurried, worried look at Philip. He disappeared back into the woods.

Neil pulled his car up alongside mine. 'Where is he?' he asked gruffly as he got out and came up to me.

'I don't know what you're talking about.'

He grabbed me. His fingers dug into my arms. He shook me violently. 'Don't play games with me, Jennifer. You must tell me where he is.'

'You're hurting me,' I groaned, prying his fingers from my arm.

He refused to unhand me. 'I know you are meeting him. This is Philip's car,' he said, glancing at the sports car. 'He's here somewhere. You had better tell me. It's urgent.'

'I don't know where he is,' I lied, glancing quickly toward the trees. I couldn't see Philip, but I knew he was there waiting, watching, listening.

'For God's sake, Jennifer. Don't lie to me. It is the last night of the full moon. Philip is particularly dangerous on nights such as this.'

'Let me go. You and your ridiculous superstitions.'

'I don't intend to leave here until you tell me where my brother is. I know he is planning to meet you. Theresa heard him telephone.'

'Then if Theresa heard his telephone conversation, she obviously knows that I planned on meeting Philip at the castle, not here. I merely stopped here to collect a few more of my things from upstairs.' I nodded toward Carlotta's villa. I hoped against hope he would not think to ask how I intended to get inside.

'How did you get Philip's car?'

'Philip left his car in the village for me.'

'Philip is dangerous. And he is not at the castle. He ran off before dinner. Are you sure you are telling me the truth? You did not plan on meeting here?'

'No, we did not plan on meeting here.'

Neil studied me for a moment. Then he said, 'I believe you.' He shook his head. 'Philip must have gone into the village. It is possible that he got a ride from someone.'

'Perhaps Philip went to see Carlotta.'

'Yes, that is possible. Perhaps he thought he could get to town before you left for the castle, or perhaps he planned on meeting you on the road.'

'Perhaps,' I readily agreed. I wanted him to go away. I wanted him to leave before Philip's presence was somehow discovered.

'Come with me. You must not stay here.'

I wrenched free of him. 'You can't boss me around like a child.'

'I do not have time to argue with you,' he said. 'Philip is most likely near the village by now. I must telephone the hospital and the police to be on the alert for him. He must not be allowed near Carlotta. In his present frame of mind, it is impossible to imagine what he is capable of doing.' He gave me a look of annoyance. Then he sighed, resigning himself to my stubbornness. 'If you intend to collect some of your things, do it, but do it quickly and come to the castle. I will wait for you there.'

He hesitated, debating with himself. Then, knowing he had very little time to do what he had to do, he got back into the limousine and sped away.

I sighed with relief and turned toward where I'd seen Philip disappear. I waited until the sound of the limousine's motor died away in the distance.

'It's all right, Philip,' I called softly. 'He's gone.'

Philip stepped out from the trees. He stood for a moment looking to the right and left. Then he started toward me. He walked with a strange gait, I suddenly noticed. It wasn't the boyish, springy walk I was accustomed to seeing, but a stooped, furtive kind of walk, like a cautious animal who'd just escaped its cage.

When he stepped into the gleam of the headlights I saw that his face was different somehow, too. His eyes were darker, his mouth slightly open. His fingers curled and uncurled as he came near me. His expression was hard and cruel.

I took a step backward as he came and stood in front of me. I hardly recognized him.

'So you got rid of him,' he said. His voice was also different. He spoke low in his throat, almost in a growl. I'd heard that voice somewhere before.

'We've got to get out of here, Philip,' I told him. 'You heard Neil. When I don't show up at the castle, he'll know you're with me.'

'Then you are finally deciding to come away with me?'

'Of course,' I said, eyeing him suspiciously. He was speaking so strangely. 'I just want to get a few things out of the villa. How do you suppose I can get inside?'

'The usual way,' he said.

I didn't understand. The strange, rasping voice kept haunting me. And his expression was so odd. There was no trace of movement anywhere on his face when he spoke. It was as if he were talking from behind a mask. His eyes stared intently at me. His whole appearance was unnerving.

'The usual way?'

'You remember. Carlotta always left the door to the fruit cellar open. How quickly you forget, Angelica.'

'Angeli — ' Suddenly I remembered. It was the same voice that threatened me in my bedroom! My hand suddenly went to my throat. *Don't show fear*, a voice kept telling me. *Don't show fear. Don't fall apart. Humor him.*

'You're getting your ladies mixed up,' I said. 'Remember me? I'm Jennifer.'

'You think you can still torment and

241

tease me, don't you? I saw you with Neil again. You prefer him to me just because he controls the money. You will never go back to him, Angelica. I will see to that.'

His eyes were blazing. I took a few steps backward. He reached into his pocket and pulled out several long wooden matches, and looked up at the moon. 'The moon is on fire,' he said.

As if in a trance, I looked too.

'That is how I know it is time,' he said. He scraped his thumbnail across the tip of one of the matches. It flared up. 'When I see fire on the moon, then it is time for fire here on earth.' He threw back his head and laughed — laughed up at the moon.

The laugh ended as abruptly as it came. He tilted his head and studied me for a moment as though seeing me for the first time. He took a step toward me. I backed away. I collided with the side of the sports car.

'Do you remember the first night we met, Jennifer? You said then how much you enjoyed fire. It did so much for a room, you said. Remember, Jennifer?'

He called me Jennifer now. The first night we met . . . Yes, it was at this very villa, in that room just beyond the blackened walls. He'd lighted a fire in the fireplace. We were having cocktails. Now I remembered seeing the strange expression on his face as he knelt there staring into the fire. I thought he'd looked strange then — but it had been a fleeting strangeness.

'That is why you love me. We both have fire in our blood. We are alike. You belong to me.'

The cold, hard metal of the car pressed into my back. I tried to inch away from him. He reached for me. His hand tightened on my wrist.

'Come. We can go through the fruit cellar. Just like old times. Carlotta is away.' He laughed again. 'Stupid old Carlotta. She thinks I am in love with her. Can you imagine, Jennifer? Carlotta believes me to be in love with her. But Carlotta has served our purpose, hasn't she?'

Philip's grip was like iron. I didn't want to let myself think about what a fool I'd been. Philip was insane, but I'd learned that too late. I had to think. I had to get away. I had to find Neil. Oh, what an utter, complete fool I'd been.

'It's all right, Philip,' I said gently, trying to pacify him, trying to coax him into loosening his grip. 'We'll go away, Philip. They'll never catch us. We'll go to the Algarve.'

'No,' he growled. 'Neil will know. He found us there before.'

'All right. Not the Algarve, Philip. We'll go wherever you say. Come. Let's get in the car and get away. Neil might return and find us. We must hurry, Philip. We must hurry.'

'Yes,' he said. 'We must hurry.' His grip finally loosened on my wrist.

He reached around me and pulled open the car door. I stepped around the door, pulling it with me as I skirted it. Then with as much strength as I had in me, I pushed the door hard against him. The blow was weak. It only made him stumble off-guard. He was knocked backward a little ways but the force of the blow did him no harm. He staggered but immediately regained his balance. He started toward me again.

I turned and ran blindly into the darkness. I ran as fast as I could, trying not to listen to his racing footsteps behind me. I couldn't do anything except try to outrun him, which I knew was impossible.

I ran to the edge of the terrace. I heard him yell, 'Angelica!' He was close, too close. A tall potted cypress stood at the very corner of the terrace. I grabbed it as I passed and pulled it over. I toppled it just as Philip passed it. I chanced to look back over my shoulder. He was sprawled under the cypress, struggling to get to his feet, fighting to free himself from the prickly branches. I didn't hesitate. I raced around the corner of the villa and started for the cliff.

I reached the back terrace and saw the wooden steps leading down. I heard Philip yell again, 'Angelica!' I hesitated. He came around to the back of the villa. I darted toward the darkest part of the terrace and crouched beside the balustrade. Philip didn't see me. He stopped and started slowly toward where I was hiding. He kept calling my name — her name — softly over and over.

Through the supports of the balustrade, I could see the long wooden stairs leading down to the beach. I slipped off my low-heeled shoes and waited until Philip was looking away from me, searching the shadows. I tossed the shoes over the balustrade and heard them clatter down the wooden steps.

Philip spun around and faced the stairway. He ran to it and started down. I dashed out of my hiding place and ran, stocking-footed, around the opposite corner of the villa. I couldn't see. I stumbled and fell. My hands and knees scraped against the loose gravel. I groaned with pain.

Philip's steps stopped on the stairs. He'd heard me. He started back up.

I got to my feet quickly and raced toward the door of the fruit cellar. Perhaps once inside I could barricade myself in a room somewhere, a closet — anywhere. Neil would come back. I knew he would. I prayed he would.

I pulled open the door and crawled down the steps into the cellar. I banged the door shut after me. I was in pitch blackness. I searched for an inside bolt. There wasn't any.

I tumbled down the stairs and staggered across the dirty cement floor. The place was damp and cold and musty. My breathing was forced, labored. I knew I couldn't run much further. I heard Philip open the cellar door. A stab of moonlight silhouetted him against the night sky.

I cowered in a corner, groping, feeling my way along the wall. My hand touched a wooden bannister. Keeping one eye on Philip's silhouette as he started into the cellar, I stealthily crept up the stairs in my stocking feet. I tried to keep my feet placed at the far ends of the steps to avoid any possible creaking noises.

I reached the top of the stairs. My hand fastened on the doorknob. I turned it quickly. The door was locked. I panicked. Philip laughed when he saw me at the top of the stairs and started up toward me.

18

My fingers brushed against something smooth and heavy — an old fruit jar.

Philip was almost at the top of the stairs. I smashed the jar into his face. He yelped in pain and fell back and I heard the railing crack as he crashed against it and toppled to the side.

The door of the fruit cellar yawned open. The light of the full moon made a path for me to follow. I bolted down the steps, stumbled across the cellar and up the stairs into the night. I heard Philip yell and start after me.

Pebbles dug into my unprotected feet as I rounded the corner of the villa and dashed toward Philip's car. If only I could get to the sports car and start it before he caught up with me.

I jumped behind the steering wheel, twisted the key and pumped the accelerator pedal. The car groaned but the motor didn't catch. Philip appeared around the side of the house. He was crouched and running at me, preparing for the kill. Again I twisted the key. The motor nearly caught.

Philip made a lunge for me. Then headlights swept up the drive. I was barely conscious of Neil pulling Philip away from me. I vaguely heard distant sounds of scuffling.

Beside the car, Neil and Philip were wrestling each other. Neil, being the stronger, had the advantage. He hit Philip hard on the jaw. Philip staggered back, banging his head against the windshield of the sports car. He slumped to the ground.

Panting, Neil stood over him with clenched fists. Philip just lay there, his eyes closed. He looked totally unconscious. Neil came to me quickly, picking me up in his arms.

'Are you all right?' he asked worriedly.

'Yes,' I managed to stammer. Then I started to cry.

He carried me to the limousine and placed me gently on the front seat. He bent over me, stroking my hair, saying soft, soothing words.

The night silence was suddenly broken by the sound of the sports car's motor starting up. We turned quickly to see Philip behind the wheel. The tires dug into the gravel as he gunned the motor and sped away. Neil called his name. Philip merely threw back his head and laughed. He swerved to make the turn at the end of the drive. The rear of the car crashed against the gatepost but Philip kept going, streaking away into the night, laughing hysterically.

Neil sighed deeply and hung his head. He stayed like that for several minutes, until the sound of Philip's car had vanished into the quiet of the night. Then he raised his eyes and looked at me.

'This is the worst he has ever been,' he said sadly.

'Shouldn't we go after him?'

'There is no need. I have already telephoned the police to be on the lookout for him. They know his car well. They will stop him wherever he goes.'

'What will we do?'

'There is nothing to do. Come, we'll go

back to the castle and ask Theresa to fix us some tea. And we will wait.'

I looked up at him. I saw the marks Philip's fists had left there. 'Your face,' I moaned. 'Oh, Neil. I'm so sorry.' The tears came again without warning. 'If only I had listened to you.'

'There, there, Jennifer. Don't blame yourself.' He tested the soreness of the bruises on his face. 'A few more marks on my face make little difference. And it is I who should apologize. I handled the whole situation very badly from the beginning.' He touched my hair, patted it, then went around the car and slipped in behind the wheel. The touch of his hand seemed to wipe away my tears. 'I should have told you the truth right at the start,' he said. 'I should have told the truth years ago.'

'You mustn't blame yourself.'

He shook his head as he started the car. 'There is no one else to blame. I knew Philip had told a different story to Carlotta. She always resented me. She felt that I was responsible for keeping Philip from marrying her. She never could

251

accept the fact that Philip was using her unkindly. I tried to tell her, but she turned against me and has resented me ever since for my interference.'

'Carlotta was in love. It is difficult to listen to common sense when a person's in love,' I said.

I saw him smile faintly and give me a knowing look. 'Yes, I know,' he said.

I flushed slightly.

'But I do not blame you, Jen. I am not the friendliest of men, nor the handsomest,' he said, touching the scar on his cheek. 'And you had both Philip and Carlotta to turn you against me. No, I do not blame you.'

We drove slowly back to Alenquer Castle.

'But I don't understand any of it,' I said, as I tried to relax against the seat. My body was still trembling. 'Surely Carlotta knew Philip's true condition.'

'No, we kept Philip pretty much under guard during the full-moon cycles. Both Theresa and I watched him closely. Even Angelica never suspected. Sometimes, during the full moon, Philip would behave perfectly normally, but at other times it became necessary to lock him up in the castle. When you came to visit Carlotta it was unfortunate that he associated you with Angelica. In his mind you are Angelica, come back to life.'

'But he behaved so beautifully the first night I arrived.' Suddenly I remembered again the strange look on his face when he had knelt staring into the fireplace in Carlotta's lair.

'Unfortunately, when he returned home that night he set fire to one of the rooms in the castle — Angelica's room. Luckily Theresa smelled the smoke and we were able to control the fire before it did much damage.'

'Why did he set fire to Carlotta's villa?' I wanted to know.

'Because you were there. Remember, in Philip's twisted mind you were Angelica again. He wanted to destroy her and the place he associated with his rendezvous with her. I heard Philip climbing down the trellis after we locked him in. I saw him to go the garage and drive away with the can of gasoline. By the time I arrived

253

at the villa, he had already set the place on fire. I found Philip running away. We fought on the lawn. He hit me with the gasoline can and stunned me enough to make good his retreat back to Alenquer Castle. That was when I went up the back service stairs of the villa to try to save you and Carlotta, but you had already managed to get out through the front.'

'But Philip was at the castle when you drove us there later.'

Again Neil nodded. 'Yes, smiling, affable Philip was there to lend a helping hand. We quarreled bitterly that night, but he merely laughed. I warned him to stay away from you both, but he was not himself; he did not know what I was talking about. In his mind I was still fighting him for the love of my wife.'

'But why did he push Carlotta down the stairs?'

Neil turned his head when he heard the telephone ringing inside the front hall. It stopped. Theresa obviously had answered it.

'Philip was afraid Carlotta would tell you there was insanity in the Alenquer family — in me — and it might frighten you off. He felt he had to be rid of her before she could ruin his chances of marrying you. But when he saw Carlotta and you at the top of the stairs, his mind clicked again and he saw you as Angelica. He became rattled, I suppose, and decided to try to destroy Carlotta and Angelica. I cannot know exactly how his mind worked, but I suspect it was something like that.'

We stopped under the portico. Theresa suddenly came rushing out of the castle. She looked extremely upset.

'What is it, Theresa?' Neil asked quickly, going to her.

'The police,' she said breathlessly. 'They called. It is Philip.' Tears were running down her cheeks.

I let myself out of the car.

'What about Philip?' Neil demanded.

'His car — ' Theresa broke down into a torrent of sobs.

Neil took her by the shoulders and shook her gently. 'Tell me, Theresa. What about Philip's car?'

Through her tears she managed to say, 'The police . . . they saw Philip's car plunge over the cliff just a few miles from here.'

I stared first at Theresa then at Neil. None of us spoke for a moment. I heard only my heart pounding and Theresa's sobs.

Neil's hands dropped away from Theresa's shoulders. 'Then it is finished,' he said sorrowfully. He sighed deeply. 'It is for the best.'

'They have asked that you come,' Theresa said, continuing to cry. 'My poor, poor little Philip,' she wailed. She buried her face in her hands and wept bitterly.

'Now, now, Theresa. Do not upset yourself until we know all the facts. Philip may still be unharmed. I must go and see. They will be waiting for me.'

Theresa suddenly straightened up. 'Is it possible Philip may be all right?' she asked. The look on her face said she wanted to believe it, but knowing the cliffs, she realized there was little likelihood of Philip having survived the crash.

'It is possible,' Neil reassured her.

'Then I must go also,' Theresa said. 'I want to be with poor Philip. He was like a son to me.' She gave me a pleading look. 'He always came to me when he was a little boy. He was not always bad. He was a good boy.'

'Yes, Theresa,' Neil said softly. 'He was a good boy.'

'It was the sickness — the moon sickness,' she said, trying to convince me of Philip's goodness, a goodness I too knew was there when his mind was sound.

I smiled reassuringly at her. 'I know, Theresa,' I said.

'I must go,' Neil announced, easing her away from him.

She clung to him. 'Take me with you, Senhor Neil. Please. Philip will need me to be with him.'

Again Neil patted her tenderly. 'But you must stay with Senhorita Carter,' he told her. 'We cannot leave a guest alone.'

'No, please,' I put in quickly, recognizing the grief, the deep concern on Theresa's face. 'I'll be all right, Neil. Really I will.'

Theresa looked up at Neil hopefully. Her gaze melted his resistance. 'Very well, then,' he said to her. 'Come along.' He glanced at me. 'We will not be long,

257

Jennifer. Have some brandy and try to relax until we return.'

'Don't worry about me, Neil. I'm fine now.'

Theresa hurried away to get a wrap.

Neil came to me. I didn't resist him when he pulled me into his arms. 'You are a very brave young woman,' he said. 'I only wish things had turned out differently for you.'

I knew he was referring to Philip. 'As you said,' I told him, 'perhaps it is all for the best. I thought I was in love with Philip. But, as you reminded me, I might have been looking for a substitute for Andrew.' My eyes got misty. 'I don't know, Neil. I'm not sure about anything anymore.'

'I wish you were sure about me,' he said softly, touching his lips to my hair. The heat of his body was comforting. I forced myself away from him. One moment I had been in Philip's arms, promising to many him, now I felt drawn to Neil. I wasn't being fair to Neil or to myself. I couldn't lean on the first man who offered to protect me from the cruelties of the world. I'd have to push Andy completely out of my life. I knew that would take time, but regardless of how long it took it had to be done.

I suddenly felt I could now go home and face the well-meaning friends who would pity me. And I could face Andy. I would see him again, just to prove to myself that everything was finished and in the past. I'd made a mistake running away. I should have stayed and stood my ground with him. I had allowed him to frighten me into hiding — and being frightened, I'd thrown myself at the first eligible man who had offered me the promise of new happiness.

I had to admit to myself that I didn't truly love Philip. I'd let myself fall under his spell. It was a challenge — a challenge to me, after Andrew, to see if I could get another man to fall in love with me.

I looked up at Neil. The scar on his cheek looked less pronounced. He saw me looking at it and touched his fingers to it.

'I only wish I were as handsome as Philip.'

'Don't say that, Neil,' I told him. 'You must never feel self-conscious about that scar. It's a part of you. It makes you the man you are.'

He tried to take me in his arms again but I resisted. 'No, please,' I whispered as I eased out of his embrace. 'Don't, Neil. Please. I don't want to discuss it now. I'm so mixed up about everything.'

'I understand,' he said patiently. 'I can wait. Only remember this, Jennifer. When I first met you I knew the danger you would find yourself in with Philip. That's why I took Carlotta's message and went to the airport to meet you. I told Theresa not to mention the message to Philip. I wanted to frighten you away. I did not want to see you go away, but I had to make you go before something terrible happened. Do you understand that?'

'But you had never seen me before. How did you know Philip would involve himself with me?'

'Philip is Philip. You are not the first girl whom I have had to protect and scare off.' He sighed. 'Unfortunately, Philip chose the same afternoon to pay a social call on Carlotta. He had not seen her in a long while. It was just one of those unfortunate coincidences.' He paused and looked down into my face. 'Do I still frighten you, Jennifer?'

I smiled at him. 'No, you don't frighten me at all, Neil.' Our eyes locked together. 'And I am grateful for everything you have done for me.'

'I do not want your gratitude,' Neil said. 'I want your love.'

My eyes drifted away from his. 'Please don't confuse me any more than I am, Neil. Please.'

'Then take your time. As I said, Jennifer, I can wait.'

Theresa had changed into a black dress, black stockings and shoes. She carried a black shawl. In her mind, she was going to a funeral. I watched them go. My body felt heavy and tired. Every muscle ached and for the first time I realized that I was in my stocking feet and my ankle was throbbing painfully. How strange, I thought, that during those moments of panic seemingly important things like shoes and sprains, hurts and fears, all flee from one's mind.

Fear is a powerful narcotic, and it is so fleeting. Once what has frightened you is gone, it is over — and yet it can possess you in an instant. I hardly remembered the panic I had felt in the fruit cellar or Philip's hands around my wrist, squeezing. Now that I thought of it, my wrist hurt. I rubbed my fingers over the marks I knew were there.

I entered the salon and went toward the refectory table with its display of decanters and glasses. I tipped some brandy into a snifter, then seated myself before the fire and let the quiet of the castle embrace me. The flames flickered and danced, making long, dim patterns on the walls. I suddenly hated the fire. I felt I'd never again feel comfortable before a roaring fireplace.

I leaned back in the chair and stretched my feet out in front of me. I toyed with the brandy glass, staring at the amber liquid swirling like a tiny whirlpool. I thought of Carlotta. Her villa was in ruins; her love was gone. Now, seeing everything as it truly existed, it was difficult to understand why Carlotta had allowed herself to be so completely blinded by Philip's charm. In spite of myself I smiled. I, too, had been totally blinded by his charm. Philip Alenquer was the kind of man a woman found difficult to ignore — especially a lonely woman.

I tried to forget the evil in him and forced myself to think about our dinner at the taverna in the Algarve, our stroll in the garden, his proposal, his romanticism, his gaiety, his love.

'No,' I said aloud, sitting up straight and shaking my head. I would not repeat with Philip the mistake I had made with Andy. I would not dwell on the happy times. I must look at reality for reality's sake. I would not continue to live in the past, to live only for the good times. Philip was insane. I would not — must not — let myself forget that fact. My view of his insanity had indeed been brief, but I'd seen it and I could not let the happy moments overshadow the truth.

I tingled when I thought of Neil's touch, but I couldn't be so hasty in that respect either. I couldn't throw myself into another entanglement. I'd rushed into Philip's arms all too eagerly. Yet I could almost feel the warmth of Neil's body, the touch of his mouth on mine when he kissed me.

No, I thought. I must be sure this time. I would go back home to where the trouble started and straighten myself out before I came back to Neil — if I came back to Neil. I had been hasty and stupid; the thought of it shamed me.

Just as I stood up I heard a click. I turned quickly to see the door to the terrace open.

'Neil,' I said.

'So you were expecting Neil,' the rasping, menacing voice replied.

'Philip!' I gasped.

19

'Surprised to see me, Angelica?' Phillip asked. 'Did you think me dead? Did you think you were rid of me at last? As you can see, I sent my car to its death without me.' He laughed low in his throat. 'Those stupid fools. They will be looking for me for quite a while before they discover I was not in that car.'

His eyes glinted in the dark. The light from the fireplace gave him the look of Satan himself. 'I could not go without you, Angelica, my sweet. I know how you would grieve for me.' He stepped closer. I cowered away from him. 'Or do you still prefer Neil to me?' The leer on his face vanished and he scowled at me. 'They preferred Neil also. They doted on him — and see what it gained them. Fire. I burned them alive on their yacht and sent them to the hell they deserved. My mother was like you — weak and stupid and blind to all of Neil's faults — and my father was no better. I gave them their just reward.'

I threw my brandy into his eyes and rushed headlong into the foyer. I tried to make it to the front door, but Philip was too fast for me. He grabbed my arm and pulled me around, sending me sprawling across the marble squares.

I pushed myself up and started to crawl toward the stairway. He was on me in a rush. His hand went over my mouth, the other hand at my throat as he pressed himself down on me, flattening me to the floor. I wasn't conscious of what I did. I heard him scream in pain and pull back when I sank my teeth so hard into his hand I tasted blood. He howled like a wounded animal. I kneed him in the groin and he rolled off me, curling up in an agony of pain.

I got to my feet and started up the stairs. I didn't know how I was to escape from there, but I had to get out of his reach — to hide if possible until Neil and Theresa returned.

At the top of the stairs I glanced back. Philip still writhed with the pain I'd

266

inflicted on his groin. I was sure he hadn't seen where I'd run. A heavy drapery hung at the top of the stairway, flanking the entrance to the corridor on the right. I hid myself behind it.

'Angelica,' Philip called, straightening himself and getting unsteadily to his feet. 'You cannot escape me, Angelica. You belong to me. You will not stay here. I will kill you before I will give you back to Neil,' he roared.

He was turning in circles down below me, searching, trying to decide in which direction I'd disappeared.

I could feel my heart pounding, and it seemed to stop beating completely when I saw Philip turn and start toward the salon. I eased out of my hiding place. He was standing in the doorway calling for Angelica, his back to me.

I had to chance getting to the door. I started down the steps, trying to move as quickly as possible. My ankle was paining me terribly but I had to get to the front door and out into the night.

I froze in my tracks when I heard a crash, followed by a hideous laugh. A light blazed up. I saw flames lick their way across the carpet of the salon. Philip suddenly reappeared in the doorway. He had a burning log he had dragged from the fireplace. He kicked it into the center of the foyer and stood over it, glaring up at me with terrible eyes.

'So you prefer to die on the staircase,' he yelled. 'Too bad your dear Carlotta is not with you. But do not fear, Jennifer. I will silence her. I'll not fail again in my attempt.' He started toward the stairs. The flames in the salon grew higher, brighter.

I turned and ran back up the steps. This time I did not stop to hide myself behind the curtains. I raced down the hall, bumping into tables and chairs, trying doors. The first door was locked. The second opened onto darkness. I slammed the door shut and threw the bolt. I backed away from it and tried to accustom my eyes to the dimness. I stumbled against a piece of furniture. My hand came away gritty, as though I had touched burnt wood. I stood there, listening, waiting. The moon cut a path across the room and I saw that I was in a bedroom — one I'd never been in before. But the furniture smelled charred; a distinct smell of smoke hung in the air.

Philip rattled the doorknob. I froze. 'Your bedroom will not protect you, Angelica,' he yelled.

I heard a loud, dull thud. The walls shook. Philip was ramming something heavy against the door, trying to break it down. I remembered stumbling against a long table in the hall. I knew Philip was using it now as a battering ram. I tried to find an avenue of escape.

The French doors opened onto a small balcony. I hobbled out onto it. I was too far above ground. There were no vines, no trellises, nothing to assist me in a climb down. I was trapped.

The ramming continued. I heard the wood begin to splinter. Philip continued to yell Angelica's name.

The door cracked and flew open. Philip stood silhouetted in the light from the hall. I could hear the crackling of flames, smell the distant smoke. A sudden choking nausea came over me. Philip started into the room. I hid myself among the tattered curtains of the four-poster bed.

'You are in here somewhere,' he growled. I held my breath. 'Your precious Neil will not be able to wash away the evidence of this fire,' he said. 'Your darling Neil will only find our ashes, Angelica — yours and mine. We belong to the fire. We will join it now. You and I, Angelica — just you and I together, forever.'

He prowled the room, searching for me. I heard him scrape a wooden match on a smooth surface. The tiny light of the match betrayed my hiding place. Philip stood there for a moment, staring at me. He suddenly seemed relaxed, calm. The tenseness was gone from his face, but evil still glinted in his eyes. Casually he picked up a kerosene lamp and lighted its wick. He held the lamp high.

'Just like old times, yes, Angelica?' he said. He placed the lamp on the night table. 'Behold your bier,' he said, making a sweeping gesture toward the bed. 'Shall you be my Brunhilde, Angelica? I will surround you by fire and keep you safe from all mortal beings. Come, my lovely Valkyrie,' he crooned. 'Come and let Wotan protect you forever.'

He made a quick lunge at me and his hand gripped my wrist as I tried to get away. He pulled me across the bed. I struck out at him with my hands and feet as I tried to jack-knife toward the far side of the bed, the side closest to the door.

The hallway looked brighter. Billowing smoke was making it difficult to breath. Philip lunged after me, upsetting the night table when I skidded away from his hands. I bounded across the room. A heavy chair went flying, crashing to the floor, tripping me as I ran.

I crawled as quickly as I could toward the open door. The smoke was less pungent on the floor. I heard a crackling sound behind me and looked over my shoulder. Philip stood staggering beside the bed. The trappings were on fire. He was beating out the flames that licked at his pant legs. Philip yelled something again but I was too intent upon my escape to listen.

The flames ran, crept, curled, rippled along the bed hangings. They licked their

271

way up and over the canopy in huge gulps of fire.

Philip cursed as I hurled myself out of the room into the smoke-filled corridor. I saw the draperies at the top of the staircase catch fire. I turned and ran, limping, toward the far end, knowing that there was no possibility of my escaping down the blazing, burning stairs.

At the end of the hall were tall latticed windows. I picked up a chair and flung it against them. The glass splintered and the fresh night air pulled the smoke toward it.

I heard Philip call for Angelica again. He appeared in the center of the hall, moving toward me through the smoke-filled corridor, like the devil emerging from hell.

I stood at the broken casement, looking down. There seemed at first to be no way of escape except to throw myself headlong into the garden. I looked out and saw a narrow ledge that ran around this face of the castle. It was my only chance. I stepped out onto it, clinging precariously to the cracks between the stone blocks.

Philip appeared in the broken window. He watched me as I inched my way along the ledge, then he tried to climb out onto the ledge. I was sure the ledge wouldn't hold the weight of both of us.

From the garden below I heard a hoarse shout. Philip heard it too and looked down. 'Stay out of this, Neil,' Philip yelled. 'You will never have her again.'

I didn't see Neil but I heard his voice telling me to hang on. A shattering, crashing sound was followed immediately by more crashing, thudding sounds. When I glanced down I saw Neil had picked up several rocks and was throwing them at Philip, forcing him back away from the casement window and the ledge.

'Hang on, Jennifer,' Neil called. 'Try to move to the drain pipe. It will support you until I can get to you.'

I was petrified. The wind tugged at my skirt, and my ankle hurt more than ever as I tried to support my weight with only my toes. I knew I couldn't hang on much longer. The strength was leaving my fingers; my legs were beginning to buckle.

Yet with some last reservoir of strength I inched toward the heavy drain pipe at the corner of the castle wall.

Philip had disappeared. From inside the castle I could hear him roaring for Angelica.

I heard a scraping sound and looked down. Neil was hoisting a ladder up against the castle wall. He placed it within easy reach. I eased myself toward it and stepped down on the top rung. Neil was climbing up from the bottom. His arms went around my waist as he pressed himself against me.

'Rest on me,' he said softly. 'I will take care of you now.'

I lay back and felt his arms go around me. Slowly he made his way back down the ladder, holding me tight with one arm. Theresa rushed at us when Neil laid me on the damp grass.

'Take care of the senhorita,' he told Theresa. He started away.

'No, Neil,' I yelled. 'You mustn't go inside. The entire lower level and upstairs are on fire. You can't save him now. Philip is trapped.'

'I must try,' Neil said as he ran, leaving me to collapse against Theresa's sturdy body.

Flames licked their way out through the windows. Far above us I heard a demonic laugh. We looked up. Philip was standing at a window, laughing up at the moon. Flames were all around him.

Neil came running back. We pointed. Up at the third-floor window, Philip was engulfed in fire. He seemed to feel no pain as he stood, hands on hips, laughing madly at the moon. A crashing sound enveloped him and his laughter turned into a horrible, hellish scream. He sank and disappeared into the flames as the ceiling collapsed on him.

I screamed and covered my face.

Theresa blessed herself and sank to her knees. The sickening sound and smell of fire filled the night. A cloud passed over the face of the moon, erasing the illusory fires that burned there.

'Come,' Neil said, gently easing me up into his arms. 'There is nothing we can do now.'

Theresa was weeping. She staggered

after us as we walked slowly away from the blazing castle. 'Oh, Senhor Neil,' Theresa moaned, looking back at the tall towers of flame, the spewing cinders, the billowing smoke.

'Do not look back, Theresa. Let it burn. It was never a happy place for us. Let the painful memories die in the ashes.' His voice was choked with sorrow. 'Let it burn, Theresa,' he repeated. 'Let it burn.'

Theresa wept softly into her hands. I leaned against Neil and felt the freshness of the night wash over me like the coming of a new day.

★ ★ ★

As the airplane slipped away from the coastline, I stared out at the peacefulness that crowned the sea. The calm, blue waters rolled steadily toward the bleached sands. Like those waters, I too wanted to go back to the shore. I didn't want to leave Portugal, but I knew it was best. Carlotta had insisted; Neil too had insisted, because deep in his heart he knew, as I did, that I would return.

Even Theresa had urged me to go. 'You will feel better for some time away,' she said.

We had patched up our differences. 'You drugged me that last day in the palace,' I said frankly to her. 'That was one of the reasons I ran away.'

She was shocked by the accusation. 'But no, senhorita, I did no such thing. I brought you tea and warm milk. Only . . . ' She paused. 'Senhor Philip was in the kitchen while I was preparing your tea. Perhaps he changed things then.'

The more I thought it, the more logical that seemed. Theresa, innocent in all the machinations that had swirled about us, would have no reason to drug my food — but Philip was another matter.

'Never mind,' I said, giving her a quick embrace. 'That's all in the past now.'

The plane banked, giving me a last look at the Portuguese shoreline, the sun glinting almost blindingly off the crystal waters. The day matched my mood perfectly. The sky was gray, the sun a misty ball above the clouds. A brisk wind seemed to hold the plane back, as if hampering my departure.

As the plane granted me that last view of the lovely Portuguese landscape, a tear ran down my cheek. 'I'll be back, Neil,' I promised. 'And when I do, it will be forever.'

I kept that promise.

THE END

We do hope that you have enjoyed reading this large print book.

Did you know that all of our titles are available for purchase?

We publish a wide range of high quality large print books including:
Romances, Mysteries, Classics
General Fiction
Non Fiction and Westerns

Special interest titles available in large print are:
The Little Oxford Dictionary
Music Book, Song Book
Hymn Book, Service Book

Also available from us courtesy of Oxford University Press:
Young Readers' Dictionary
(large print edition)
Young Readers' Thesaurus
(large print edition)

For further information or a free brochure, please contact us at:
Ulverscroft Large Print Books Ltd.,
The Green, Bradgate Road, Anstey,
Leicester, LE7 7FU, England.
Tel: (00 44) **0116 236 4325**
Fax: (00 44) **0116 234 0205**

Other titles in the
Linford Mystery Library:

THE SILVER HORSESHOE

Gerald Verner

John Arbinger receives an anonymous note — offering 'protection' from criminal gangs in exchange for £5,000 — with the impression of a tiny silver horseshoe in the bottom right-hand corner. Ignoring the author's warning about going to the police, Arbinger seeks the help of Superintendent Budd of Scotland Yard. But Budd is too late to save Arbinger from the deadly consequences of his actions, and soon the activities of the Silver Horseshoe threaten the public at large — as well as the lives of Budd and his stalwart companions . . .

A MURDER MOST MACABRE

Edmund Glasby

Jeremy Lavelle, leader of the esoteric Egyptian Society the Order of the True Sphinx, has illegally purchased an ancient Egyptian mummy. Watched by his enthralled followers, he opens the coffin and begins to unwrap the body . . . The head is that of an ancient scribe, his shrivelled and desiccated face staring eyelessly up from his coffin — yet from the neck down, wrapped up in layers of bandages, are not the mummified remains which they had expected. Instead, they stare in horror at the decapitated corpse of a recently killed man!

NEMESIS

Norman Firth

A burlesque beauty's fierce yearning for vengeance is triggered following the callous shooting of her younger sister in a gang war. Rita's single-handed efforts to avenge her sister's death bring her into contact with some of gangland's most ruthless killers, whose animal instincts cause them to treat life cheaply, and women callously. Through many dangers Rita pursues her determined way towards the clearing of the mystery surrounding her sister's slaying, and the vengeance which has set her whole being aflame . . .